"You know I don't have any money,"
Jacob told Samantha.

She frowned. "What's money got to do with anything?"

"You can't ask a girl out for coffee."

"What have you got against coffee?"

"You know what I mean. You need money to ask a girl out on a date, Miss Sherman."

Samantha winced at both his formality and his point of view. "I would have thought a man like you was too old for girls, Jake." She figured he was about thirty. His face had a mature, lived-in look, except on those rare occasions when he smiled.

"That's Jacob," he said.

"And I'm Sam."

A reluctant grin tugged at his lips. "I'll make a bargain with you. You call me Jacob, and I'll call you Sam."

"Just so you call me," she said with a flirtatious look.

Dear Reader,

This month we have a wonderful lineup of books for you—romantic reading that's sure to take the chill out of these cool winter nights.

What happens when two precocious kids advertise for a new father—and a new husband—for their mom? The answer to that question and *much* more can be found in the delightful *Help Wanted: Daddy* by Carolyn Monroe. This next book in our FABULOUS FATHERS series is filled with love, laughter and larger-than-life hero Boone Shelton—a truly irresistible candidate for fatherhood.

We're also very pleased to present Diana Palmer's latest Romance, *King's Ransom*. A spirited heroine and a royal hero marry first and find love later in this exciting and passionate story. We know you won't want to miss it.

Don't forget to visit that charming midwestern town, Duncan, Oklahoma, in *A Wife Worth Waiting For,* the conclusion to Arlene James's THIS SIDE OF HEAVEN trilogy. Bolton Charles, who has appeared in earlier titles, finally meets his match in Clarice Revere. But can Bolton convince her that he's unlike the domineering men in her past?

Rounding out the list, Joan Smith's *Poor Little Rich Girl* is a breezy, romantic treat. And Kari Sutherland makes a welcome return with *Heartfire, Homefire*. We are also proud to present the debut of a brand-new author in Romance, Charlotte Moore with *Not the Marrying Kind*. When the notorious Beth Haggerty returns to her hometown, she succeeds in stirring up just as much gossip as always—and just as much longing in the heart of Deputy Sheriff Raymond Hawk.

In the months ahead, there are more wonderful romances coming your way by authors such as Annette Broadrick, Elizabeth August, Marie Ferrarella, Carla Cassidy and many more. Please write to us with your comments and suggestions. We take your opinions to heart.

Happy reading,

Anne Canadeo
Senior Editor

POOR LITTLE RICH GIRL
Joan Smith

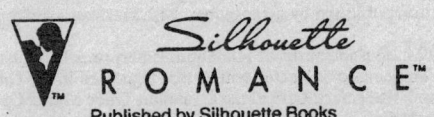

Published by Silhouette Books
America's Publisher of Contemporary Romance

If you purchased this book without a cover you should be aware that this book is stolen property. It was reported as "unsold and destroyed" to the publisher, and neither the author nor the publisher has received any payment for this "stripped book."

 SILHOUETTE BOOKS

ISBN 0-373-08972-4

POOR LITTLE RICH GIRL

Copyright © 1993 by Joan Smith

All rights reserved. Except for use in any review, the reproduction or utilization of this work in whole or in part in any form by any electronic, mechanical or other means, now known or hereafter invented, including xerography, photocopying and recording, or in any information storage or retrieval system, is forbidden without the written permission of the editorial office, Silhouette Books, 300 East 42nd Street, New York, NY 10017 U.S.A.

All characters in this book have no existence outside the imagination of the author and have no relation whatsoever to anyone bearing the same name or names. They are not even distantly inspired by any individual known or unknown to the author, and all incidents are pure invention.

This edition published by arrangement with Harlequin Enterprises B. V.

® and TM are trademarks of Harlequin Enterprises B. V., used under license. Trademarks indicated with ® are registered in the United States Patent and Trademark Office, the Canadian Trade Marks Office and in other countries.

Printed in U.S.A.

Books by Joan Smith

Silhouette Romance

Next Year's Blonde #234
Caprice #255
From Now On #269
Chance of a Lifetime #288
Best of Enemies #302
Trouble in Paradise #315
Future Perfect #325
Tender Takeover #343
The Yielding Art #354
The Infamous Madam X #430
Where There's a Will #452
Dear Corrie #546
If You Love Me #562
By Hook or By Crook #591
After the Storm #617
Maybe Next Time #635
It Takes Two #656
Thrill of the Chase #669
Sealed with a Kiss #711
Her Nest Egg #755
Her Lucky Break #795
For Richer, For Poorer #838
Getting To Know You #879
Headed for Trouble #919
Can't Buy Me Love #935
John Loves Sally #956
Poor Little Rich Girl #972

JOAN SMITH

has written many Regency romances, but likes working with the greater freedom of contemporaries. She also enjoys mysteries and Gothics, collects Japanese porcelain and is a passionate gardener. A native of Canada, she is the mother of three.

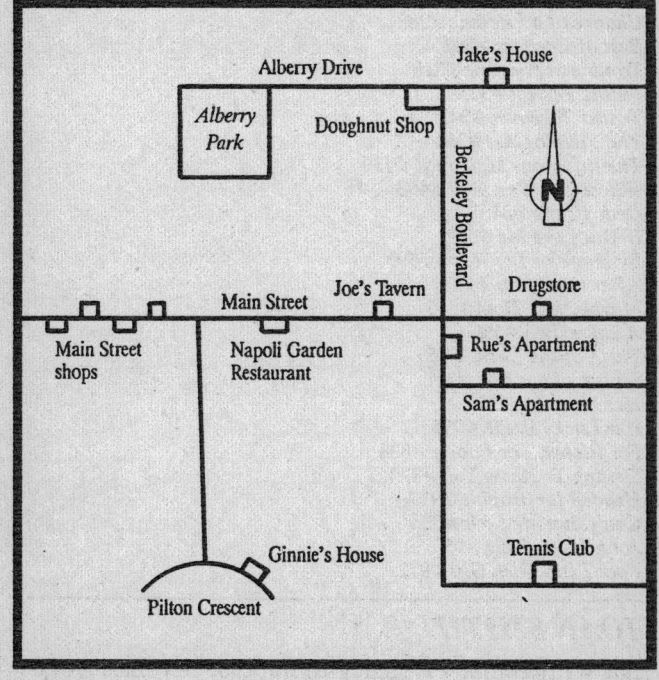

Chapter One

Samantha Sherman sat at her mirror, trying to decide whether to let her hair grow or give her hairdresser another easy twenty-five dollars. Antonio said she should keep it short, but a gorgeous black lace dress in the Nearly New Boutique window was shouting "Take me home!" every time she saw it.

Sam—everyone called her Sam—wore her coppery hair very short with a side bang. Those monthly visits to Antonio's for a trim added up. There were cheaper hairdressers in town, of course. On the other hand, Antonio did a really great job. Since her hair was ruler straight, all the upkeep it needed was shampooing and brushing. The short cut also showed off her collection of earrings. At last count she had sixty pairs.

If it weren't for the big white hoop rings she was wearing at the moment, she would look like a teenager. The smattering of freckles across the bridge of her short nose accentuated the impression. Her face was heart-shaped, tapering to a small, determined chin. Her deep-set green eyes looked almost too big for her face.

The ringing of the phone in the next room brought her musings about her hair to a stop. She jumped up and darted to the living room, nearly tripping over a sneaker she had kicked off at the bedroom door. Sam always preferred to go barefoot when she could, and the peachy wall-to-wall carpeting in her apartment was an added incentive. The deep wool pile felt as warm and soft as sheepskin curling around her toes.

"Hi, Sam here," she said.

The greeting was the compromise she had worked out to solve the little complication of running her business out of her apartment. It sounded strange to say, "Let Sam Do It," if it was a personal call. But as that was the way her shopping service was listed in the yellow pages, she wanted to let her callers know they'd reached the right number.

"I'm calling about your ad in the newspaper," a man's voice said. It was a deep, strong voice.

She smiled. Men were good customers. They weren't as finicky as women. They often called to have her select a gift for their mothers or for their wives or female employees if they were busy businessmen. The younger men seemed to prefer buying their own gifts, but she had helped a few furnish their apartments. Sam had soon discovered that a professional shopper did a lot more than just shop. During her three years in the business she had done everything from give advice to the lovelorn to help a young bride throw her engagement party. And she'd enjoyed every minute of her work.

"Yes, sir. What can I do for you?" she asked.

"I'm setting up an office and I need a desk," he said bluntly. Men did that, got right down to business, she thought. A man who was setting up an office needed a lot more than a desk, although he might not have realized it yet. He'd need chairs and filing cabinets, maybe a carpet and lamps. All sorts of smaller items. "I'm new in town and pretty busy. Could you get one for me?"

"I certainly could. Why don't I come over to your office and have a look at it to give me an idea what sort of desk would suit you?" And to see what else you need, you poor lost lamb, she added to herself.

"That'd be very good of you. I'm at 13 Alberry Drive. Do you know the area?"

As a three-year resident of Findley Falls, Sam knew the town pretty well. She was a little surprised that the address wasn't in the commercial part of town. It was in a middle-class residential suburb on the northern edge.

"Yes, I know it. When would it be convenient for you to meet with me?"

"The sooner the better."

Sam glanced at the Cartier tank watch on her wrist, a graduation present from her father. "I can be there in fifteen minutes," she said.

"Great. I'll be waiting for you."

"Whom shall I ask for?"

"Jacob Foster. I'll meet you at the door."

"I'll be right there."

She hung up the phone, a frown pleating her brow. Alberry Drive seemed a funny place to be setting up an office, but that was Jacob Foster's business. Maybe that area was going commercial. She hadn't been there for a few months. A decent desk could cost anything from five hundred to the moon, depending on how luxurious the office was. It could be a good commission for her, and well worth the drive.

She took a quick glance at herself in the mirror before leaving. Since Jacob sounded like a young man, she didn't think he'd object to the outfit she was wearing. You could wear jeans anyplace, and her blue cashmere sweater lent them a touch of class. After all, she wasn't a lawyer or business consultant, trying to impress anyone. Shopping for hours on end, you liked to be comfortable. She wiggled back into her sneakers, slung her big leather pouch bag over her shoulder and headed out of her apartment.

The sight of her little white minivan always gave her spirits a lift. Let Sam Do It—Personal Shopping Service was painted in fuchsia on the side panel, to provide advertising as she went about her business. If the items to be purchased were not too bulky, she delivered them to her customers personally. She smiled as she remembered some of the unlikely things her van had carried. Everything from six piñatas and dozens of balloons for a big birthday bash to a dozen yew foundation plantings and ten peony bushes for old Mr. Soper, who loved gardening but couldn't get out to the nurseries.

Sam had gone back that evening after-hours and helped Mr. Soper plant the trees. When the peonies bloomed, he had invited her over to see them. He had served her lemonade and given her an enormous bouquet from his garden. It was those little personal exchanges that she particularly enjoyed about her work.

She drove through the familiar streets of Findley Falls, a medium-size town in upstate New York. She had thought she'd be working in a clinic in some large city when she graduated from college with a sociology degree. That was some dream! It seemed half of the students in the States were sociology majors. She had sent out fifty-odd applications, got half a dozen nibbles, and zero offers. Although she'd done pretty well, she wasn't a straight-A student. There had been too many distractions at college to give it her best effort.

She had been on the basketball team and the debating team and, of course, had a full social life. Sociology wasn't exactly what she had thought it would be, either. In her naïveté, she had thought the study of social institutions and social relationships would involve work with people, but it had mostly involved studying the work of other sociologists. Sam liked being with people.

When she hadn't landed a job, her dad had suggested she take some other course. She turned that offer down, as well as his offer to go back home to live with him and be his secretary. She didn't want to be a legal secretary any more than she wanted to go back home. Her dad was very understanding about it. At times she almost thought he was relieved. He had given her the van and enough money for a couple of months. She wanted to be on her own. She knew that when young people lived at home they were still considered children. It was time to stand on her own two feet.

One of the things she liked about Findley Falls was the small-town feel of it. She used to visit her grandparents there. She had lived two years with them after her mom died. Once she had gotten over the tragedy of the death, they had been the happiest years of her life. Her grandmother had treated her like a daughter, taking more interest in her school and her friends than her own mother had. Not that she blamed her mom. Her mom had a busy life of her own, with a big house to see to, plus the lavish entertaining her father's work involved. Her dad had to do a lot of traveling that year. He was a corporation lawyer, and the company he worked for was opening an office in Europe.

Findley Falls was big enough to have such amenities as theaters and even an art gallery. When Sam discovered it didn't have a professional shopper, she was in business. Shopping was what she did best. Her grandparents were dead now, but she had kept in touch with her old high school friends and had soon made new friends, as well.

Large old trees lined the side streets as she weaved her way north. It was late May; patches of blue sky still showed between the lacy boughs of fresh young leaves. A riot of tulips and daffodils bloomed everywhere. Hugh clouds of yellow forsythia added a touch of spring against the brick houses. As she turned on to Alberry Drive, the real estate became less impressive. The houses were smaller and closer together; the flowers were fewer and farther between. She read the street numbers. There it was, number thirteen. An unlucky number, if you believed in superstition. It was just a small white aluminum-sided house, two stories high, with no business sign or anything.

She pulled into a graveled driveway and went uncertainly to the front door. What kind of office could this be? Some sort of business that was run out of a house, obviously. Her dream of a big commission dwindled. There was an expensive sports car in the driveway, however. Maybe this area *was* going commercial. As she approached the door, it opened and a man called to her.

"Are you from the shopping service?"

"That's right," she said, smiling to see she had at least reached the right place. "I'm Sam."

She bounced up the steps. A studious-looking young man in wire-rimmed glasses shook her hand. He seemed a little surprised at her casual clothes. "I'm Jacob Foster, the man who called you. The office is right in here."

As she followed him into a virtually empty house, Sam noticed his broad shoulders and trim body. He had the graceful stride of an athlete. Like her, he wore jeans and sneakers. The only suggestion of the businessman was his shirt. It was a tailored one, sky blue, rolled up at the sleeves. She had noticed one of those little plastic pouches in the pocket, to prevent his ballpoint pens from leaking on his shirt. His long hair was the shade of ripe wheat and curled at his collar.

A trunk, a bunch of cardboard boxes with papers spilling out the tops and a couple of suitcases sat on the floor of the living room that he planned to use as his office. The room had slatted blinds and a wall-to-wall carpet in a strident shade of blue. Against one wall a door was placed across two piles of bricks to form a desk. The makeshift desk held two computers, printers and various plastic cases of disks. A wooden crate sat at the terminal of one of the computers. He had doubled a sweater up on it to act as a cushion. The computer was on, with a bunch of figures on the screen.

"This is going to be my office," he announced with just a touch of pride in his voice. When he reached up and removed the glasses, she saw his eyes were a deep Wedgwood blue. He had the rugged look of an outdoor person—a weathered face, with a strong nose and squared jaw. "Eyestrain," he explained, motioning to the glasses. "I've been working overtime."

That sounded promising at least. If he had lots of work, he must have lots of money.

"Then you'll certainly be wanting a proper desk," she said, smiling at the door and bricks. "What style did you have in mind for your office? Will you be doing it in modern decor?"

He blinked. "Are you an interior decorator?" he asked, in a voice of horror.

"No, I'm a professional shopper."

"Oh, good. You gave me a bit of a scare there. I can't afford a fancy decorator." When he smiled, he looked about ten years younger and a lot more handsome. He had a cute, lopsided grin. "I just want a good, solid desk, strong enough to hold my computers. I've measured out the space I'll need. Six feet long should do it, and four or five feet deep."

A desk that size would cost plenty! And it didn't seem Jacob was going to be very fussy. "Any other requirements? I mean as to metal or wood—"

"Not metal. It rattles when the printer is working. I kind of like oak. Oh, just one more thing. It can't cost more than five hundred bucks."

Sam tilted her head and looked at him with a wry grin. "Dream on," she said bluntly. "An oversize oak desk would cost a couple of thousand."

"That much!" He raised a shapely hand and wiped it across his chin. "Well, I guess I could go to one *K*."

"Say what?"

He blinked in confusion. "What? Oh, pardon me. *K* stands for kilo which stands for one thousand. Trade jargon." He grinned apologetically. "I guess the budget could go to a thousand dollars."

It still wasn't enough for a new desk like that, but Sam was beginning to feel sorry for Jacob Foster. That plastic pouch in his shirt pocket holding three ballpoint pens suggested he was a nerd. There was only one way to go.

"Do you have any objection to a used desk?" she asked.

"No, that'd be fine. In fact, I like old things. They built them to last in the old days."

"Then we're in business. I'll scrounge around the used-furniture stores. Wouldn't you be more comfortable with a chair? And you'll need some filing cabinets for your papers." She glanced at the floor, where folders spilled from the boxes like lava from a volcano.

"I can't afford all those frills just yet. Just a desk for now."

Sam hardly considered a chair a frill, but she didn't want to embarrass him. "Okay, I'm off."

"There's one more thing," he said uncertainly. "Er—how much do you charge, Miss—"

"Sam, my name's Sam. I charge five percent."

He nodded. "That's not much, for all your work."

"No, it isn't. I know all the merchants in town. I usually get stuff at the dealers' prices, since I do a lot of buying. I charge my customers retail, so I make up something there." But for secondhand furniture she didn't think there'd be a special price.

"How soon do you think you'll get my desk?"

"I just left," she said. "With luck, you'll have it today. Will you be in this afternoon?"

"I'll be here all day. Do I give you a check or something?"

"It'll be C.O.D. You can pay me my commission when you've examined it and are sure you're satisfied."

He smiled that lopsided smile again. "That's not very businesslike," he said. "What if I don't pay you?"

"Then you get a call from my lawyer," she said demurely and walked out.

Sam didn't bother visiting the fine antique stores. As she drove downtown, she pondered whether to go straight to the junk shop, or to give Lou's Furniture a try first. Lou took trade-ins and carried a large line of office furnishings. He might have something. She decided to try Lou Vincent. Within minutes, she was pulling into the alleyway behind his store. She had done enough business with Lou that she knew her way in by the back door, through the store room. It was piled high with old sofas and chairs, dining room tables and sideboards, and the castoffs of dozens of households.

Lou heard her and came into the store room. "Oh, it's you, Sherman," he said with a scowl.

Lou Vincent was the only person in the whole world who called her by her last name. At five foot three, he was two inches shorter than Sam. His hair had dwindled to a little black fringe around the edge, like a monk, but his flashing eyes suggested an unmonkish interest in her. She had never seen him without a foul-smelling cigar in his mouth. He wore his usual outfit, a navy blue vest hanging open over a soiled white shirt, and shiny blue trousers that matched the vest.

"Hi, Lou. Do you happen to have a big old wooden desk in stock? It has to be a real whopper. Six feet long. And it has to be cheap. Five hundred bucks." She always gave a lower price than she expected to pay.

"They don't make desks like that no more."

"I don't want a new one."

"Are you sunk to buying secondhand, Sherman? You ought to get into a legit business, a nice girl like you."

She had lost the *girl* battle. "The pot calling the kettle black?" she said, her eyes roving over his secondhand merchandise. "My business is strictly legit."

"The office merchandise is in the corner," he said and led her to it.

There were dozens of desks, most of them metal, none of them six feet long. There were also filing cabinets, assorted tables and several padded swivel chairs that would be more comfortable for her client than a wooden crate. Maybe if she could find two identical desks, Mr. Foster could push them together and make one very long one.

"Nothing bigger, huh?" she said.

"I do have one whopper, but I couldn't let you have it for five hundred. I want a thousand for it. It's solid oak."

She looked up, interest sparking in her green eyes. "Maybe we can make a deal," she said.

"No deals. It's a gift at a thousand. Here, I'll show it to you. I don't keep it here with this junk."

He led her to a different corner of the room. The desk was exactly what Mr. Foster was looking for. A solid oak, double pedestal desk with drawers down either side, a little over six feet long and about four and a half wide. It would hold an elephant, never mind a couple of computers and printers. Sam suppressed her admiration.

"It's pretty battered looking," she said, examining the surface, where a few minor dents and scratches marred the surface.

"In the furniture business, we call it distressed," Lou said. "They do that to new furniture now to make it look antique. Beat it with chains and put dark shoe polish in the dents."

"Would you take seven hundred for it?"

"Not a penny under a thou. I'm firm on this one, Sherman—even for you." He gave her an oily smile.

When Lou said he was firm, he meant it, but she might still get a few perks thrown in. "I'd take it, except that my customer needs a chair, too, and a couple of filing cabinets for his office."

"Maybe you'd like me to throw in a fridge and stove and a free car while you're at it," Lou said, to show his opinion of that.

Sam knew perfectly well that Lou loved to haggle. She also knew that since Lou had so many of those wheeled desk chairs and cabinets, they must be a glut on the market.

"My customer already has a car," she said with a grin. "Sorry we can't do business. I guess I'll just have to keep looking around. See you again some time, Lou." She turned to leave.

Lou let her get to the door before calling her. "I must be crazy!" he said. "All right, I can let you have a chair, but that's it."

Sam shrugged. "Sorry. My client needs two filing cabinets."

When she left half an hour later, she had gotten a swivel chair, a side table with wheels to hold computer paper and two filing cabinets thrown in for the original price of the desk. Both she and Lou were happy with the bargain. She arranged for delivery at three that afternoon and left. Her car phone rang while she was on her way back home. She picked up the receiver.

It was an unusual request. That was one of the things Sam liked about her job. You never knew what would come up next. In this case, an elderly gentleman had died, and his widow wanted Sam to go and pick out a coffin. Mrs. Kelly couldn't get about much, and she feared the funeral parlor was trying to talk her into a grander coffin than she could afford. She wanted her husband buried as he had lived, decently but not extravagantly. Sam visited the woman in person to discuss the requirements in detail. This was too delicate a job to do by phone.

She spent the remainder of the morning and the early part of the afternoon working for the new widow, who also wanted a black dress and hat for the funeral. There were some minor shopping chores as well—wine and some catered sandwiches and cake for the relatives who were coming from out of town for the funeral. It gave Sam a good feeling, to be able to help someone in need. She stayed with Mrs. Kelly, listening to her reminiscences, until her sister arrived from Philadelphia.

At ten to three, she headed back out to Alberry Drive. Sam wanted to see Mr. Foster's expression of delight when he saw the bargain she had got for him. She arrived five minutes before Lou's van and outlined what she had done.

Jacob Foster was mad as a wet hen. "But I only wanted a desk! I told you money is tight," he said angrily. "You've exceeded your authority, Miss—"

"Just call me Sam," she said, gritting her teeth at his lack of appreciation of her haggling.

"You must have another name."

"Sherman, if you must know, but my customers all call me Sam."

"Sherman, like the tank," he said, with an accusing look. Personally, he thought Miss Sherman should have been called after a bulldozer. How dare she go buying things without his consent? He should have known better than to hire a kid. "I'm afraid I can't accept delivery of items I didn't ask you to buy."

"The dealer was firm on a thousand for the desk. I got the rest of the stuff thrown in free," she explained patiently. "Just wait till you see it. You'll love it. And when you're ready to furnish the rest of the place, I can get you bargains on house furniture, too."

It would be a cold day in hell when he used her services again. "Very kind, I'm sure," he said, with an ironic lift of his eyebrow.

But when the desk came, Jacob was enchanted with it. He had to admit the other things would come in handy, as well. He ran his hand over the honey-colored desk surface, then pulled out a drawer to examine the construction. "This is solid oak!" he exclaimed. "Not just veneer."

"Tell me about it," Lou said, wiping the perspiration from his brow. "It weighs a ton." He and his assistant could hardly carry the huge desk. "I must be crazy! I wanted to keep this beauty for myself, but my rent happened to be due, and Sherman twisted my arm. You got yourself a real bargain here, Mr. Foster."

Jacob turned an apologetic look on Sam. "No, Miss Sherman got me a real bargain."

He paid Lou, who left, still muttering that he must be crazy. Sam waited to get her commission.

"That's fifty dollars I owe you, Miss Sherman," Jacob said, handing her the money. "You really did a great job. You're a smart shopper."

"I've had plenty of experience." She smiled. "And as I mentioned, I can do just as well for you when you're ready to furnish the house. Will you be living here, or will it all be offices?"

Jacob didn't think it was any of her business, but he replied, "I'll be living here. I won't be furnishing the place for a while yet."

"I guess you'll want a bed at least, and maybe a sofa and chair and TV," she suggested.

"I don't watch much TV. I have a stereo, and now that I have this swanky chair," he said, giving the seat a whirl, "I don't need a sofa."

Sam looked around the unfurnished room. "Where will your guests sit?" she asked.

"I don't expect I'll be having many guests for a while. I'm new in town. I don't know anyone."

"You know me," she said.

"Yeah, and you know I don't have any money."

She frowned. "What's money got to do with it?"

"You can't ask a girl out for just coffee."

"What have you got against coffee?"

"You know what I mean. You need money to ask a girl out on a date, Miss Sherman."

Sam winced at both his formality and his point of view. "I would have thought a man like you was too old for girls, Jake," she said. She figured he was about thirty. His face had a mature, lived-in look, except on those rare occasions when he smiled.

"That's Jacob," he said.

"And I'm Sam."

A reluctant grin tugged at his lips. "I'll make a bargain with you. You call me Jacob, and I'll call you Sam."

"Just so you call me," she said with a flirtatious look. Then she turned to leave, tucking her fifty dollars into her purse.

Jacob watched her as she left with a feminine sway of her slender hips. He had been alone in the empty house for two days. Sam was the only person he had spoken to, other than Lou and the waitress at the nearest hamburger stand. He didn't mind being alone as long as he had his computer, but suddenly he didn't want Sam to leave.

He didn't seem to get along very well with most girls—*women*. He'd have to remember that. Really Sam looked more like a girl, with her hair chopped off short and her jeans and grungy sneakers. Her face was young, but to judge by her body and her self-assurance, she wasn't exactly a kid. In any case, she wasn't the snooty kind who insisted on fancy restaurants. In fact, she looked about as poor as he was. If she were doing well, she'd get her hair done properly and wear better clothes like the businesswomen he met. And she had practically asked him to ask her out. Maybe she was lonesome, too.

"I really like the desk, Sam," he said. "Thanks for finding it."

She looked back over her shoulder, then stopped walking. "It'll look great once you get it polished up."

"Yes, I'll have to get some furniture polish."

"I have some in the van," she said. "I keep it to give stuff I'm delivering a final shine. Shall I get it?"

"If you're not in a hurry."

"I'm not."

She darted out to the van, and Jacob stood looking after her. Poor kid. If he was the only customer she'd had that day, she wasn't making much. And she didn't seem to have any other customers to rush off to. Fifty bucks a day would hardly pay her rent. She probably lived in a room some place.

She was back in a minute with the polish and a rag. She planned to polish the desk herself, but Jacob reached for the polish and began to work on the desk. He worked calmly, efficiently. His strong hands stroked the oak lovingly, bringing it to a high gloss.

"This is beautiful," he said, in a reverential tone. "It almost seems a shame to cover all this oak with computers. They don't make things like this nowadays. It'll be here long after I'm gone. An heirloom, really."

Sam looked askance at the desk. It was big and strong, but hardly her idea of an heirloom. It didn't have any fancy carving or elegant brass pulls like her dad's desk. It seemed to suit this Jacob Foster, though. Strong, well built, with no frills. She watched him a moment, then said, "Well, it's time for me to split."

"Oh, don't go!" Jacob said. She looked at him, surprised. "I thought we might go and have that coffee," he said. "If you're not busy, I mean."

"Like I said, I'm free. There's a donut place on the corner. They make good coffee. I promise I won't order a donut," she said, and laughed.

He grinned. "That's all right. I'm not actually penniless. You can have a donut, if you didn't have any lunch. In fact, you can have two or three."

"I don't think my waistline would appreciate that!"

His eyes went automatically to measure her waist. Her figure was sharply outlined in the tight jeans. The feminine curve of her hips and the swell of her breasts looked a little incongruous with her chopped off hair and freckles. Maybe that was what was so intriguing about her, the combination of girl and woman.

"I don't think you have to worry," he said.

They went out into the spring sunlight. "Are those your wheels?" she asked, pointing to the sports car.

"Yeah, bought in the good old days, when I had a job."

"Got laid off, huh?" she said, with a wince of sympathy.

"Yeah."

"It's happening to a lot of people these days. I guess your car'll be repossessed. I mean it'll be tough to meet the payments."

Jacob looked surprised. "I paid cash for it," he said. "I'd never buy anything I couldn't pay for. That'd be foolish."

Sam just looked at him blankly. "My van's paid for too." She didn't tell him it had been a present from her father.

They decided to walk to the donut shop, since it was only half a block away. The sign in the window said, "Special Recession Fighter. Free donut with coffee. Bottomless cup."

"We're in luck," Sam exclaimed, pointing at the sign.

For some reason, Jake suddenly felt happy. He was damned near broke. He didn't know anybody in town, and he'd probably have to sell his new car, which he loved. But the sun was shining. It was spring. He was with a pretty girl—*woman!*—and the donuts were free.

"You wanted a donut all the time, didn't you?" he said, and opened the door.

Chapter Two

The welcoming aroma of freshly perked coffee filled the air. There were other delicious smells, too: cinnamon, apple and chocolate. They got their coffee at the counter and chose their donuts.

"Chocolate icing for me," Sam said at once. There was never any contest when chocolate was a choice.

Jacob scanned the donut racks. "Hmm. So many choices, so little money. I'll try the cinnamon."

They took their selections to a little table for two by the window.

"So, tell me all about yourself, Jacob," Sam said, stirring sugar into her coffee. Jacob took his with cream, no sugar.

"Not much to tell. I was working for a big software company in New York. They went belly-up, throwing me and a dozen other engineers out of work. I had just blown my life savings on that fancy car you saw in the driveway. That'll teach me to be so extravagant," he said, shaking his head in regret.

"Hey, don't be so hard on yourself! You paid cash. They can't take it away from you."

"No, but I didn't need such an expensive car. It was an extravagance," he said with a guilty frown. "Anyway, New York is ruinously expensive when you're out of work. I sublet my apartment and moved here."

"Why here, to Findley Falls? You don't seem to have friends or family here, and it's not exactly the center of industry. What did you do, close your eyes and point your finger at a map?"

"Hardly! I'm not that reckless. No, I did a survey, considered my options. Findley Falls is more or less halfway between Syracuse and Albany—two good markets. And it's not an impossible commute to New York, if I get customers there. It's a nice, civilized town. And of course the rent is cheap. I can do my work anywhere. Location isn't really important nowadays. Computers and fax and all that put you in touch with the world in minutes."

"That sounds reasonable," she said. She might have known Jacob Foster wasn't the type to take a crazy chance. "What sort of work do you do, exactly? You mentioned working for a software company."

"I'm a programmer. Software is mostly done by big companies now, but big companies have to start small. I'd like to give it a try, create my own programs and sell them. Meanwhile, my survival plan is to tailor standard programs specifically for various businesses. I have some contacts in the field, and of course I'm sending out letters all over."

Sam remembered her discouraging experience of sending out letters. "No nibbles yet?" she asked.

"Oh, a nibble here and there. Nothing firm. I've really just begun looking."

"It's tough getting established," she said, thinking of her own experience.

"Tell me about it. How about you, Sam? How did you become a shopper?"

"I was born to shop," she said, smiling to remember all those shopping trips with her mother. It was practically the only thing they did together. Her mom wasn't the kind of mother who made cookies or cleaned her own house. The servants did that. "When I ran out of money and couldn't buy for myself, I started shopping for other people."

"That sounds like a clever use of your, er, skills," he said, assuming she had no special training or education. Sam's mouth was full of chocolate-covered donut, preventing her from straightening him out at the moment.

Trying to be helpful, he added, "You know, it might be a good idea for you to take a course in computers, Sam. You can't get a good job these days if you're not computer literate. You're bright and hardworking. You could probably get a job in an office. Steady work—"

She swallowed and glared at him. "For your information, Jacob, I am not illiterate!"

"Computer literate, I said."

"I know what you said. I have a computer, and I know how to use it. I got it when I was at college."

"You went to college!" he exclaimed. She hardly looked old enough to be a graduate. She must have flunked out.

"I graduated in sociology."

"Really?"

His surprise irked her. "Did you think I was stupid or something?"

"No! Just too young to have graduated. And you're now shopping for a living! Boy, things really *are* tough," he said supportively. "One of my engineer friends is hacking a cab in New York."

Her blood temperature rose a few degrees. "You make it sound like I steal the stuff. There's nothing wrong with being a professional shopper. I'd rather do that than sit in a dull office all day."

"I'm sorry. I didn't mean to be patronizing. It's just a shame you have to do that kind of work when you have a degree. But I admire your pluck, digging in and doing whatever you have to in order to survive. This recession is having some good effects, along with the obvious bad ones. It's teaching us to fall back on our resources, toughening us up, making us get back to basics. We were becoming too fat. Consumer oriented."

Sam wasn't sure she deserved his praise. She loved her work, and was an A-1 consumer. "Actually, I like the work," she said.

"You'll find something more suitable when the economy picks up."

"Shopping suits me. Just think of all the pent-up consumer demand that's building. I'll be rushed off my feet when the next boom comes along."

"But does the work satisfy you intellectually?" he asked doubtfully.

"I'm not Einstein, Jake. See, I can't even remember to call you Jacob. There is certainly an intellectual side to my work, though. You have to know the stock of dozens of stores, and be able to spot the bargains. It involves knowing the quality and workmanship of hundreds of products. I wouldn't last long if I didn't do a good job. But mostly what I like about my work is the emotional satisfaction. I like people. This morning I helped an elderly widow arrange a funeral. She really needed someone, and I made a difference to her."

Jacob listened attentively, but with an air of uncertainty. "I guess we're just on different wavelengths. I don't think of work as an emotional thing, although I actually do love my work."

"And I love mine." She went on to tell him some of her experiences.

"I have this one client, Rue Sanderson, whose hobby is shopping. She's a very wealthy widow, lives all alone in a penthouse condo, which she redecorates every year. I think her decorator and I are her best friends. He does her house, and I buy her clothes and cosmetics and personal stuff. Oh, and she has her masseuse, of course. She comes twice a week."

"Is she an invalid?"

"Oh no, she goes out to parties and golf and things, but she doesn't like shopping in stores. The crowds, you know."

Jacob thought Sam was complaining and tried to comfort her. "Well, you have your other clients, as well, like the widow. At least it's not all spoiled society ladies."

"I like Rue, too. She's fun to work for." Sam had never thought of Rue as a spoiled society lady. What she liked about her was that she reminded her of her mom. Although now that she considered it, she supposed her mom had been spoiled.

"What do you do for fun, Jacob?" she asked, since they seemed to have exhausted the subject of their jobs.

"My hobby is computer games. Not playing them—creating them."

"Computers again? Sounds like a busman's holiday to me."

"I guess the busman wouldn't have taken a bus ride on his holidays if he didn't enjoy it. I certainly enjoy my hobby. That's why I have that second computer. It does graphics. Another extravagance."

"No wonder you were wearing glasses when I first met you. Don't you ever give your poor eyes a rest?"

"I jog, play a little tennis. I played football at college. I had to, I was on a football scholarship. It was the only way I could hope to get a college education."

"You make it sound like a penance."

"No, actually I liked it. You know, the roar of the crowd, Saturday hero, all that childish stuff." His face wore a rueful look of fond nostalgia as he spoke about his college days and touchdowns and things. Then he pulled himself back to attention. "The training took a lot of time I should have been spending on my schoolwork."

"It must have helped your popularity a lot, though," she said. "With the girls, I mean."

"Girls?" he asked, with a teasing smile.

"Women."

"Yeah, with the kind of women who were impressed with a football player," he said dismissingly. "They could be quite a nuisance actually."

Sam found she couldn't find any sensible comment to make. She had never heard a man complain about women chasing him before. "Poor you, beating the women off with clubs. My heart bleeds for you," she said.

"It wasn't quite that bad," he admitted with a lop-sided grin. Their cups were empty. "Want a refill?" he asked.

"I'd better get home and see if I have any telephone messages. I wouldn't want to miss out on a client, if it's a rush job."

They walked back to Alberry Drive. Jacob left her at her van. "I really enjoyed meeting you, Sam. I hope everything goes well for you."

"You too, Jacob. We'll keep in touch. Since you don't know anyone in town, give me a call if you're lonely. I have a TV—and a coffeepot."

"I don't want to be a parasite," is all he said. It was his eyes, and his rather sad smile, that said the rest.

Sam knew enough about men to sense that Jacob liked her, but his stupid male pride would prevent him from calling. He was a stranger in town, and she knew how lonesome that could be.

"You can bring the donuts," she said, making a joke of it. "Really, I'd like to see you again. It doesn't matter about—you know, that you're short of money at the moment. We've all been there."

"That's very kind of you, Sam. Thanks." Still, she felt he resented her kindness, or maybe it was just that he was financially embarrassed.

He held the door while she got into the van. She didn't think Jacob would call, not until he had some money anyway. To repeat her offer would seem pushy, like those college women he'd complained about, so she just waved and left.

There was a call from Rue Sanderson waiting when Sam reached her apartment at five. Rue's throaty voice conjured up an image of the forty-something widow, with her carefully tinted blond hair and expertly made-up face. Her body, despite the masseuse and the golf, was a little bigger and softer than fashion decreed. That was certainly different from Sam's mother. She had never let an ounce of cellulite attach itself to her body.

"Darling," Rue said, "I've just been reading about this most divine new cosmetic. It positively removes wrinkles, and it's only fifty dollars an ounce. You must pick up some for me at the drugstore. Get me the four-ounce bottle. It's cheaper that way, only one fifty— that's one ounce free. You see, your lectures on economy are paying off." She gave the name of the product. "And while you're there, you might as well get me a bottle of Giorgio. I'm practically out. Tomorrow will be soon enough. I'm going out now. I'll be gone for the evening. A do at the golf club."

Sam thought about that order as she made her dinner. Maybe Jacob had a point. A touch of recession wouldn't do Rue any harm.

Sam opened the fridge door and peered in at her supplies. Better finish up that pastrami before it went bad. She got out rye bread, dill pickles and mustard and cut a wedge off a canteloupe for dessert. Deciding not to use the small table and two chairs in her kitchen, she put her dinner on a tray and went into the living room to watch the news while she ate.

The peach carpet set the color scheme for the room. The walls were done in a lighter hue of the same color. The love seat was a low-slung white leather, the tables glass and brass, piled with magazines and books. Modern prints and one painting were added touches to the room.

Sam had decorated it herself, using her shopping skills to contrive the best result with the minimum expenditure. She was happy with the result. As she contrasted it with Jacob Foster's living room, she couldn't suppress just a little twinge of guilt. All these nice furnishings had been paid for by her father. He was glad to do it; in fact, he had insisted. Obviously Jake—she couldn't call him anything but Jake—didn't have a rich father.

"I don't want my daughter living in a hovel, Sam," her dad had said. "You're my only child. All I have will be yours one day. I don't see why we should wait until I die to give you a little something. I'd be worried, thinking you were living in some miserable rooming house."

The 'little something' had been a check for ten thousand dollars. Out of that, she'd gotten the used van and furnished her apartment and lived until she was supporting herself. Maybe she was a little spoiled, but she hadn't taken a penny from her dad since that day. Except for birthday and Christmas presents, of course.

"Since you're such a good shopper, I'll let you buy your own gifts," he always said, handing her the check. "That's the sensible way to do it. What do I know about what a young girl wants?"

Sometimes she wished he would buy her a gift. It wouldn't have to be expensive, just something that he saw in a shop, that showed he'd thought of her. Surely a father should have some idea what his daughter would like. Sam was under no illusions about her father, now that she was more mature. He was the kind who had always been away when she was growing up. He probably gave her so much money to make up for not being there. She knew he loved her, but sometimes she wished she had had more of his time and less of his money.

She put the thought out of her mind. Seven o'clock. What should she do tonight? A phone call settled the problem for her. She went to the tennis club with friends and back to Ginnie Moore's house afterward for coffee. Ginnie was an old high school friend. She was nursing in Findley Falls and lived with her parents.

It wasn't until Sam reached home at eleven-thirty that she thought of Jacob again and wondered what he had done that night, alone in a strange town. He mentioned he played a little tennis. She could have invited him as her guest—or would that make him a parasite?

In the morning, Sam went to Rue's before going to the drugstore. Rue's apartment was a lavish, sprawling penthouse in the Regency Tower, the priciest condo in town. This year she had it decorated in art deco. Rue looked anachronistic in a pink exercise suit, complete with leg warmers and a sweat band. "I'm going to start doing exercises," she said. "I have an instructor coming at nine. Isn't that fun?" Naturally Rue couldn't buy an exercise videotape and exercise by herself. She never liked to be alone.

Rue had added a few items to her shopping list. "I'm having a party tomorrow night. I want you to buy me some fresh flowers. Lots and lots of daffodils. I'll wear my new yellow gown."

"Do you need any special foods?" Sam didn't do ordinary grocery shopping, but for special clients and special occasions she provided that service as well.

"No, I'm having it catered, dear. Oh, but you might stop in at a travel agent and get me some brochures on Paris, if you don't mind. I love Paree in the spring. Mimzi Harcourt and I are thinking of darting off to France."

Rue's errands didn't take long. With an hour free and her pockets jingling, Sam decided to buy the black lace dress in the Nearly New Boutique. She often shopped there, where they had such interesting old clothes. This one was from the flapper era. It had a long waist and a short full skirt that flirted enticingly about her knees. The black lace contrasted dramatically with her ivory skin and red hair. Her hair was just about the right style, too. She'd wear a band around her forehead, like the flappers did, and maybe a long strand of pearls.

The clerk found her a band for her hair. Sam wasn't sure she'd ever have the nerve to wear the getup in public, but it would be great for a masquerade party. She put the bag in the back of her van and went home to have lunch and check her answering machine. A Mr. Hewitt wanted her to call at his office. When she went, she learned he wanted patio furniture—a table with umbrella and six chairs. He gave her a sample of the colors he wanted—dark green and white, to match the awnings on his house.

"Good quality, mind you. I don't want those plastic woven things. Something with cushions. I'm entertaining the president of my company at home this weekend. Since my wife passed away, I have to do these things myself. My secretary won't even bring me a cup of coffee or bring my newspaper, much less do my shopping," he grumbled.

"A price range?" Sam said. Mr. Hewitt wasn't the kind of man who wanted to waste any time.

He gave her the figure and said, "If they can't have it delivered by Friday, I'm not interested. I need the furniture for the weekend. And I don't want to have to do any assembling. I'm a busy man."

At the price he had quoted, Sam didn't think the supplier would balk at assembling the table, if assembly was required. She'd gladly slide the cushions on herself.

She went to the best patio furniture store in Findley Falls and took her time selecting what she thought Mr. Hewitt would like. She passed on the cute, curlicue, white wrought iron furniture. His office was furnished with heavy, square furnishings. She selected massive white aluminum patio furniture, with striped cushions in hunter green and white and took a brochure with pictures of it back to his office to save a return if he didn't like it.

"That's exactly what I want!" he said and actually smiled. "It'll match my awnings. I wasn't sure they made such a thing nowadays. I went to one place yesterday, and everything was pink and yellow. As if a man would want pink furnishings. I'll keep you in mind next time I need something for my house or office, Miss—"

"Sam. Sam Sherman."

"You might keep an eye out for a good leather sofa, the kind with buttons on the back, in chestnut. For my new office," he said, his chest swelling with pride. "I have just been made vice president, with my own sitting room. I won't have a decorator in here wasting my time. I'll be in touch when I need it. Good day. See my secretary about your commission."

It was late afternoon by the time Sam had done a little scouting for the leather sofa. Her answering machine had no more messages, so she decided to drop in on Jacob Foster and see how he was doing. Since she was hungry, she took some donuts with her. Jacob could supply the coffee, so he wouldn't feel like a parasite.

When she tapped at the front door, Jacob answered so quickly she thought he must have heard her van drive up.

"Sam!" he exclaimed, with a surprised smile of pleasure. He was wearing a T-shirt this time, with no nerd's pocket protector. She wondered where his pens were. The shirt was stuffed into the waist of his jeans, emphasizing his board-flat stomach. He wasn't wearing his glasses.

"Hi, I was just nowhere near the neighborhood and decided to drop by," she joked.

"I'm flattered. Come on in."

"I come bearing gifts," she added, holding the box of donuts up by the string.

"Our spirits must be in sync. I just made fresh coffee."

He led her into the office, where the oak desk now had pride of place, with the computers and printer assembled on top. There were still a few boxes around the edge of the room, but there was no paper coming out of them. As the tops of the filing cabinets were piled high with folders, she assumed Jacob was doing his filing when she interrupted him.

"Hey, this is begininng to look like a real office," she said.

"Yeah. I really love that desk. All I need now is clients. I'll get the coffee."

"Can I help?" she asked, and followed him to the kitchen.

"Cream's in the fridge," he said. She noticed he had a package of paper cups and plates on the counter. He carefully poured the coffee into the paper cups. "Sugar's in the cupboard," he said.

When Sam opened the cupboard, she saw a box of crackers, a few cans of soup and one of beans and such bachelor fare. The beans especially made her feel sorry for Jacob. She wanted to make him a nice home-cooked meal. The kitchen was bare, except for an electric kettle and the fridge and stove that had come with the house. There was plenty of space for a table and chairs, but the room was empty. A venetian blind hung forlornly at the window. The fridge was nearly empty too. He had milk, eggs, half and half, butter and a bag of apples.

"Don't mind the look of the place. As you know, I'm baching it," Jacob said over his shoulder. "I mean to buy some dishes one of these days."

"Didn't you bring anything with you from New York?"

"My computers. Oh and some blankets, a sleeping bag, a pillow, stereo," he admitted. "I was sharing a place with a couple of guys. I left most of the stuff with them. I figured dishes would only break, and besides, there wasn't room for them in the van. My friend lent me his minivan—for my computers and stereo. We'll take this into my office. You can have the chair," he said.

Sam sat on the chair and looked at the computer screen. Expecting to see columns of figures, as she had seen the day before, she was suprised to see an animated figure that looked like a medieval warrior. A Viking, maybe. He had a sword and a funny hat with horns on it.

"Jacob Foster!" She laughed. "Have you been wasting time playing computer games? And here I've been feeling sorry for you."

A boyish blush suffused his face. "I told you it was my hobby. I made up that game. The Franks versus the Visigoths. I didn't waste the whole day," he rushed on to assure her. "I printed up that pile of inquiry letters."

A neat stack of filled envelopes sat on the desk, waiting to be stamped. "How does this game work?" she asked.

"I'm just making it up now. We can't play it on that computer. But I have a Game Boy, if you're interested." His flashing eyes suggested that he was very much interested.

He got the game, and they both sat on the floor, since there was only the one chair. "I'll get my pillow for you and the sleeping bag. We can make a cushion out of it," he said.

Jacob disappeared out the door. She heard his footfalls darting upstairs, taking them two at a time. He was back within a minute with the pillow and sleeping bag, which he arranged neatly on the floor.

The game was really no contest. Jacob was an expert, and Sam had only played a few times.

"I don't see why all the games are so violent," she said. "Why don't they make a computer game for women?"

"You mean something like hunting for a husband? Hmm, that could be interesting."

"You mean *choosing* a husband. They're not that hard to find," she informed him. "Half the people in the world are men. A little more than half, actually.

Since you're biologically inferior, Mother Nature evens things out by making more of you."

He cocked a grin at her. "Is that what they taught you in sociology?"

"You don't have to be a sociology grad to know that."

"The game would take some thinking. We'd have to assign values to the men, in order to keep score. Like a hundred points for Einstein."

"And a thousand for a rock star or movie star," she said, to tease him. "They make millions."

"Your sense of values is seriously warped, Miss Sherman," he riposted. "Surely you don't judge a man solely by the thickness of his wallet."

"No and not solely by his brain power, either. It's more complicated than that. Who do you think would be more fun on a date, Einstein or a movie star?"

"A movie star—say Michelle Pfeiffer, but we were talking about a marriage game. Einstein might not be much good at a dance, but I figure he'd provide better company over the long haul."

"I guess, if you're into physics. Personally, $E=mc^2$ about exhausts my knowledge of the subject. I guess it's supposed to be the theory of relativity, but I don't actually know what that means."

"Don't look at me for an explanation. Now about this game of husband hunting..."

"How about doctors and lawyers? Shall we say five hundred points?"

"Worth five times as much as Einstein?" he asked in mock chagrin.

"Maybe not Einstein. I just meant scientists in general."

"Gee, thanks," he said. "I consider myself a scientist, in a small way. Engineers are hands-on scientists. Way down there below doctors and lawyers, huh?"

Sam made a grimacing face. "I goofed. I wonder if that's what they mean by saying comparisons are odious. Sorry about that, Jake."

"That's Jacob."

"I always think of you as Jake."

He peered at her from the corner of his eye. "So you've been thinking about me, have you?"

"Oh I definitely have my eye on you." She smiled. Jake's eyes widened in interest. "When you make it big with this marriage game, I'll expect to be commissioned to buy all your furniture," she explained, and watched his eyes return to normal.

"You only build up my hopes to let me down, cruel wench. It's strictly a business friendship, then?" he asked. He spoke lightly, but she sensed a note of genuine interest.

She studied him for a minute, trying to decide whether she was imagining things. No, he was definitely interested—and she was beginning to think Jake might have potential, if she could loosen him up a little. "Not strictly. You're an interesting man. I never met a hermit before."

He shook his head. "I'm not really a hermit, Sam. I must be giving you a very strange idea of myself. It's just this business of being out of work—it really cuts the underpinnings out from under a fellow."

"I know. Men's egos are very much tied up in their jobs. Don't let it get you down. You're still just as good as when you were paid a lot of money by that company in New York. You haven't changed, the economy has."

"I try to tell myself that. Sometimes, late at night in bed, I don't seem to believe it. We'll have a special category for the unemployed male in our marriage game."

"Maybe you should make it a job-hunting game. You're not alone out there."

"But could the interested parties afford to buy the game?" he asked.

"What I actually meant when I suggested a nonviolent game for women was a shopping game."

He looked at her in mock surprise. "I guess you've never been at Bloomingdale's when they have a sale."

"Of course I have, on my buswoman's holidays. Shopping is my business. In the game, you'd get points for beating the other shoppers to the bargains. Speaking of bargains, I found one today for myself."

"What was that?" he asked, curious to hear what she had bought. It might give some clue as to her lifestyle.

"A dress. Black lace. It's gorgeous."

Jake just sat, blinking in astonishment. He couldn't picture this tomboy in black lace. Where would she wear such a thing? And it must have cost a fortune.

"Oh, that's nice," he said inanely.

"And such a bargain. Of course I got it at the secondhand store."

Suddenly Jake was smiling. He was right about Sam. She wasn't a foolish woman like that Rue person she talked about. She was just a poor, hardworking girl, who had to buy a secondhand dress. He felt so sorry for her he wanted to kiss her.

"We'll go out and celebrate the dress," he said.

"As soon as you get a client."

"We have to eat, whether I have a client or not. Shall we order a pizza?"

"Only if we go Dutch."

"I can afford a pizza, Sam."

"So can I. I made a bundle today. I insist."

"No, really."

"This is the nineties, Jacob. Women can insist now too."

They went Dutch on the pizza. While they had dinner, Jacob told Sam a little more about his work. She suggested a few potential local clients he might visit.

"Just small outfits, but it all adds up. I heard the janitor at the Regency Tower complaining that he needed a computer to keep track of the tenants' requests. Many of them are wealthy seniors who travel for months on end, leaving all sorts of instructions. You know, water the flowers on Monday, a man is coming to paint the walls on June the third, and oh yes, don't forget to phone me in England if a letter comes for me from so and so."

Jacob listened eagerly. "That would be a very simple program. Thanks, Sam, I'll give him a buzz. The Regency Tower, did you say?"

"That's right. It's on Berkeley Boulevard, just off the main street. No reason you couldn't try a few of the other apartment buildings, too, once you have the program made up."

"Maybe I could sell the program to one of the bigger software companies," he said pensively. "You really need them for the distribution."

When the pizza was gone, Sam got ready to leave. "There's something to be said for this Bohemian lifestyle," she said. "No dishes to wash. I only meant to drop in for coffee, and here it's nine o'clock. Talk about overstaying your welcome!"

"I'm glad you came. I really enjoyed your visit, Sam."

"Don't encourage me," she joked. "A good thing you already told me you don't like women falling all over you."

"Did I say that?"

"When you were at college—remember?"

"Vaguely," he said. "Lately I haven't had that problem."

"Maybe you should take up football again."

When Jacob walked her out to her van, it was dark in the driveway. Sam wondered if he'd kiss her. He opened her door and stood uncertainly a moment, as if trying to decide whether he should.

Sam didn't consider it that big a deal. She reached up and planted a kiss on the corner of his lips. "See you," she said, and turned to get into the van.

Jake's hand came out and seized her wrist. "We can do better than that," he said softly, turning her around and pulling her into his arms.

His lips brushed hers gently, tentatively, almost as though he expected her to draw away. She put her arms around his waist and squeezed lightly to encourage him. His lips firmed then, as he crushed her against him. Her hands moved over his taut back, enjoying the ripple of firm, masculine muscles, warm beneath his cotton shirt. As the kiss deepened, she could feel the thud of his heart against her breast. It was a long, sweet kiss, that held the promise of greater passion to come.

You could always tell whether that essential chemistry was there, and Sam knew it was definitely there between her and Jacob. The air seemed to quicken, her heart beat faster, and a certain magic something invaded her.

She sensed that Jacob felt it, too. She already knew he wasn't the kind of man who rushed into things. She wasn't surprised when he released her after one kiss, but she was a little disappointed. He just stood silent a moment, still holding her close, with his cheek against hers. Was the echo of those uneven breaths coming from her or him? Then he lifted his head and smiled.

"I'd better let you go now. Take care."

"See you later," she said, and slid into her van.

Jacob stood on the curb, watching as she drove away, with a flutter of her fingers out the window and a little toot-toot of her horn. He stood a moment, even after her van had turned the corner. Sam would have been surprised at the dismal expression on his face. He looked almost angry—and he was angry.

Why the hell did he have to meet a woman like that when he was in no position to start a relationship? No job, no money, not even a decent apartment where he could entertain her. A pizza, which they'd had to eat on the floor, for crying out loud! And she had paid for half of it. Sam was kind enough to say money didn't matter. Jake knew better.

You could enjoy one or two simple dates—walks, drives—but eventually a woman expected to be taken out for dinner. She'd want to go dancing, to concerts and movies. Too bad he had to meet the right woman at the wrong time, because Sam didn't seem the kind of girl who'd be content to sit around waiting.

She had actually taken the initiative in their friendship. She had hinted for a date. "Just so you call me," she had said, in that flirtatious way. She had called on him today; she'd even been the one who had initiated their first kiss. An outgoing, fun-loving woman like that—she probably had dozens of men friends.

He thought of her suggestion of a program to keep track of the needs of large apartment buildings and went back into the house. He'd get started on that first thing tomorrow. The best idea would be to talk to the janitor and see what sort of information he'd want to store. A list of tenants' names, apartment numbers, departure and arrival dates, chores to be done for each one. Really a very simple program. He'd do it in C language. It would only take a day or so, and if the program flew, he could keep the wolf from the door for a while.

Chapter Three

Sam liked to perform a few extra services for her special customers. One of those jobs was taking Mrs. Sutton's three poodles to the grooming salon every four months. That was her first job the next morning. Mrs. Sutton asked Sam to buy a wedding present for her niece while she was waiting for the dogs to be trimmed.

"Her mother suggested bed linens. I thought one of those down-filled duvets would be nice, with a cover to match the sheets and pillow cases."

"What a great present! I love mine. What color did you have in mind?"

"The bedroom is painted off-white, so she'll want something colorful, but not garish."

Sam jotted down the price range her customer was interested in and got the size of the bed. It was the kind of commission she liked—a generous amount of money to spend and some freedom of selection. She thought of the bride, about to begin her married life, and felt a twinge of regret that she had never found that perfect someone. Her job was enjoyable, she had plenty of friends, but until a woman married, there was always that feeling of something missing, of waiting, wondering.

She browsed through the bedding shops and department stores until she found a soft blue paisley matching set. She took it on approval in case her client wasn't happy with it. Mrs. Sutton was delighted, so that was all right. At eleven, Sam picked up the trimmed poodles—Eenie, Meenie and Minie. Mrs. Sutton's one joke was that she "didn't want no mo'."

Sam's afternoon was less enjoyable. A crotchety old man wanted her to buy him a typewriter. He had written his memoirs of World War Two, and was ready to start typing them. He didn't want an electric machine and he didn't want to pay more than a hundred dollars. He was dissatisfied with the small portable she showed him. It was the best she could do at his price. He accepted the second one, but Sam had a sinking feeling he'd be calling back for her to return it.

At four o'clock, she decided to call it a day. She wanted to sink into a bubble bath and pamper her tired muscles for an hour. She was just about to undress and hop into the tub when Rue Sanderson called.

"Sam, thank God I got you in person. That dinner party I mentioned yesterday—the darned caterer has got the measles! So inconsiderate. He should have another chef on standby. Here I am with six people coming for dinner. What shall I do?"

"Why don't you take your guests out for dinner?" Sam suggested. She really wanted that bubble bath.

"Oh, no. I've got the apartment looking gorgeous, with all those daffodils. And I can't wear a long dress out to a restaurant. It'd look ostentatious."

"I could buy some steaks. They don't take long to cook."

"But you have to serve potatoes or something with them. I don't want to start *cooking*."

"If you don't want to go out and you don't want to cook, then you'll have to order in. How about Chinese? The Mandarin Duck has some nice dishes."

"That's an idea! I'll order enough different dishes that everyone can find something he or she likes. I'll heat it in the microwave. Now, what about dessert?"

"That's easy. I'll pick up something fancy at the bakeshop."

"Would you? Get something really special, to make up for the horrible dinner. Maybe a mocha cake, or better yet, a tray of French pastries. Yes, I think the pastries would be nice. I'll pay your special service fee."

It was Rue who had come up with this idea. Sam often received panic calls from Rue to dash out and buy her a pair of stockings or a can of coffee. For these items on which the commission was too insignificant to pay Sam for her trouble, she charged a special service fee, depending on the amount of work involved. For selecting and delivering the pastries it would be ten dollars, but Rue probably wouldn't let her away with less than twenty. "Darling, I'd pay a *taxi* more than that!" she'd say. Rue used people, but she was extremely generous.

"I'll be right back," Sam said to her waiting tub, and she darted out to the bakeshop.

She made her selection—chocolate éclairs, individual pieces of chocolate mocha cake, strawberry shortcake and various creamy delights. They filled two large boxes. Rue might only be entertaining six guests, but she'd want more than a dozen choices.

"You're an absolute lifesaver!" Rue said, and gave her a peck on the cheek.

She took Sam in to admire her table. It looked lovely, with a white lace cloth over yellow linen, to match the vases of daffodils and her gown. She gave Sam two twenties.

"The pastries only came to fifteen dollars, Rue," Sam said. "The bill's in the box."

"Oh, darling, you saved my *life!* I'll call you tomorrow. I want to talk to you about the Paris trip. I have a few things I'll need. Oh, and would you mind dropping in on Annie Lavin before you leave? She wants you to exchange that lamp—you know, the little Italian one with the tiny light? It looks hideous in her living room. I told her it didn't match her decor, but you know Annie. She's decided on the big white one instead. The lamp store would probably exchange it for her, but they only deliver on Wednesdays and Fridays, and she insists she has to have it for tonight for her bridge club."

"I'll call on Mrs. Lavin, but this is too much, Rue," she said, frowning at the two twenties.

Rue said, "Oh pooh! It's only money. Please take it. It eases my conscience for being so selfish."

As Sam took the elevator down to Mrs. Lavin's apartment, it occurred to her that Rue had probably blurted out exactly what her parents had always done. They had given her too much money and too many things, to relieve their consciences for being selfish.

Maybe that was where she had gotten the habit of buying things when she was unhappy. She was trying to fill the hole in her emotional life with things, but it didn't work. A new sweater was no substitute for love.

Sam had known the Italian lamp would be exchanged sooner or later. Mrs. Lavin was never satisfied with her first choice. She wasn't at home, but the maid gave Sam the lamp. She trundled it down to the elevator, trying to keep it from poking other people's legs as the elevator filled up. She was just getting off at the ground floor when she heard Jacob's voice around the corner. She thought she was hearing things, then he appeared, accompanied by the janitor, Ned Reilly.

She hardly recognized Jacob at first. His T-shirt and jeans had been replaced by a very nice lightweight business suit, a white shirt and tie. His hair was neatly brushed in place. He was carrying a briefcase, and looked every inch the successful businessman.

"Jacob!" she called, and went to meet him. "What are you doing here?"

"Sam!" He looked more shocked than happy, but when he recovered, a wide smile beamed out to welcome her.

The janitor also recognized Sam, as she was a frequent visitor at the Regency Tower. Rue had found several customers for her in the building.

"Mr. Foster just sold me on the idea of a computer," Ned said. "Now I have to sell the condo management on it. I don't think there'll be much trouble. They're pretty reasonable about things. I'll be in touch with you, Mr. Foster. I think you have a darned good idea there. You've no idea how many residents I have to take care of, each with his own list of orders. I wasn't sure I could handle a computer, but you make it sound incredibly easy."

"It is," Jacob said. "I'd be happy to come and show you how to run the program."

"I'll be in touch then." Ned tipped an imaginary hat, said, "Good day," and left.

Sam turned to Jacob. "Boy, you don't waste any time!"

"I started on the program after you left last night and finished it this morning. I think I'm in business. Shall we go and celebrate?"

"Congratulations." She held up the lamp. "Unfortunately, I'm in business, too. I have to exchange this lamp."

"I'll go with you. Let me carry it."

"My van's out front in the visitors' parking lot."

When they went out, she saw that Jacob's snazzy sports car was there, but since the lamp wouldn't fit in it, they took her van. The streets were busy with workers going home after a day's work. Sam had to pay attention to traffic, but when she had parked at the lamp shop she said, "You're looking pretty stylish, Jacob. Nice threads."

"Thanks. You can't look like a beggar when you go begging. Have to keep up appearances. Old jeans and—" He came to an embarrassed halt, as he had just noticed that Sam was wearing jeans.

She noticed his embarrassment and soon realized why he had suddenly stopped. "That's all right. I'm not begging. I always dress like this. Today I delivered three poodles to their grooming shop. You can't wear heels and a skirt for work like that."

Jacob felt a wince of sympathy for Sam. He'd soon be back on track, either working for a big company or for himself, but either way, he had a good future. Poor Sam seemed doomed to do this menial work. Delivering dogs and lugging lamps around! She should aim higher.

He cleared his throat and said, "You mentioned you used a computer at college. I imagine you used it for word processing, for your essays and whatnot. With a little practice, you could brush up your skills and find an office job."

"I don't much enjoy processing words," she replied.

"I could teach you data entry. There are plenty of jobs in that field."

Sam made a derisive face. "Give me a break, Jacob. I love my work. Well, maybe not exchanging things, but I did a lot of other things today. I like the variety. I'd hate being stuck behind a desk all day. I'm a free spirit."

When she got out of the van, Jake noticed she looked hot and tired. It was hard work, whatever she said, and he resented to see her doing it. She was independent; she probably didn't like anyone to feel sorry for her. He insisted on carrying the lamp into the fancy import shop.

The clerk gave Sam a dismissing look and said, "Sorry, miss, we don't allow exchanges."

"It's for Mrs. Lavin, at the Regency Tower," Sam said. "When I bought the lamp for her, the other clerk promised it could be exchanged. I think you'll lose a lot of customers if you aren't willing to fulfill your promises."

"Ah, Mrs. Lavin! Of course. I remember now. I'll get the Italian alabaster lamp."

"Thank you," Sam said sweetly. When he left she said aside to Jacob, "Jerk!"

The little incident confirmed in Jacob's mind that Sam's life was a series of degrading hassles. The Italian alabaster lamp came in two large boxes, one for the base and one for the shade. If she'd been alone, she'd have had to carry them both, which would have meant making two trips. He took the heavier base. Even a man's strength felt the weight of it.

"You're sure you like this job, Sam?" he asked, when the lamp was stowed and they were heading back to the Regency Tower.

"Maybe I won't when I'm old and gray, but it suits me for now."

"You have to think of your future," he said. Lord, there was no future in this job. He'd have to get busy and find something she'd like, something with a future.

At the apartment building, Jacob carried the heavier box upstairs for Sam. Mrs. Lavin had returned. She was an elegant-looking woman and quite pretty, but Sam always thought she looked as though she were afraid to move, in case she'd muss her hair. It was firmly lacquered in place.

"Oh, the lamp isn't assembled," Mrs. Lavin said, looking at the two boxes as if they were objects from outer space. "Could you give me a hand, Sam?" But it was at the handsome young man that she cast a helpless look. She was a well-preserved forty-five, and by no means immune to younger men.

"Sure," Sam said, and began pulling the boxes open. The lids were held in place with big staples.

Jacob took out his Swiss Army knife, yanked out the staples and asked Mrs. Lavin where she wanted the lamp.

She fluttered and smiled. "Try it over there, at the end of the sofa," she said. "My, it's nice to have a strong man around the house. Have you taken on a helper, Sam? I don't think you introduced us."

"This is Jacob Foster. Jacob, Mrs. Lavin. Jacob isn't my helper. He's a friend—a computer expert."

"A computer expert! Very impressive! Maybe Mr. Foster wouldn't mind assembling the lamp for me. I'm no good at technical things."

"Would you mind, Jacob?" Sam asked, with an apologetic look.

"Not at all," he replied, damping down his annoyance.

While he assembled the lamp, Sam bent Mrs. Lavin's ear about the value of computers, and how the condo management would soon be asked to buy one for their janitor.

"It would help Ned keep track of all the details more efficiently," she explained. "You remember the mix-up about watering your plants when you were in Florida last winter."

"I certainly do! Ned killed my African palm. Forgot to water it."

"If he had a computer, he could have all that sort of thing on a schedule that he checked every day. Mr. Foster would teach him how to run the program. It would be very up-to-date, state-of-the-art," she said recklessly. "I know you Regency residents are always the leaders in management innovations."

"That's true," Mrs. Lavin said. The older residents liked to feel they weren't left behind in the technological revolution. "I'll certainly vote for it." She looked at the lamp and shook her head. Jacob had assembled the lamp and placed it where she had suggested. "Try the other table, Mr. Foster. Or perhaps the cabinet there by the piano. That will be closer to my bridge table."

He lugged the heavy lamp around until Mrs. Lavin was happy with it. He gritted his teeth and smiled, for Sam's sake, but he could hardly keep from telling Mrs. Lavin to make up her bloody mind. If he hadn't happened to meet Sam, she'd be doing this heavy work herself.

When they finally got away he said, "She didn't even pay you! Do you make exchanges for free?"

"Yes, it's all part of the service."

"I think you're being exploited. These women are taking advantage of your youth and inexperience."

She gave him a cagey grin. "I appreciate the youth, but forget the inexperience. I'm an old hand at this game. I just got a firm vote for your computer system. I chatted Mrs. Lavin up while you screwed the lamp shade on. It would've helped if you hadn't frowned like the Cookie Monster all the time you were there. She liked you. She'll vote for the computer, and she's the president of the condo management team this year. They take turns."

"You sly rascal!" He laughed. "But I thought I *was* smiling."

She shrugged. "What goes around comes around. We do her a favor, she does us one. I think you New Yorkers call it PR or something."

"You've earned that celebration drink. I wish I could make it a fancy dinner, Sam, but until the system is actually bought, I'm still officially unemployed. We'll have a cocktail."

"Make it a beer and you've got a date. I can't go into a cocktail bar dressed like this. I was just about to sink into a nice bubble bath when Rue phoned. That's the rich lady I told you about last night," Sam said, as she weaved her little van through the traffic.

"What did she want?" Jacob asked distractedly. A picture of Sam, about to sink into that bubble bath had popped into his head. He yanked at his shirt collar. Suddenly he felt warm.

"Her caterer got the measles. She needed help arranging her dinner."

"You cook, too?"

"Heck no. I just suggested she order Chinese, and then I dashed out to buy her some dessert."

At five percent commission, Jacob didn't think Sam had made much on that deal. "They're definitely exploiting you," he scowled.

"To the contrary, Rue is embarrassingly generous. You wouldn't believe the tip she gave me."

"I should hope so! I didn't notice Mrs. Lavin tipping you." Tips weren't the same as real pay, as far as Jacob was concerned. They were at the client's pleasure. The car engine gave a thump. "What's that noise?" he asked in alarm.

The van began making wheezing noises. "I don't know. The van does that sometimes. I think it has bronchitis."

"Sounds like your fuel injection system's in trouble."

"I have the van checked regularly. The mechanic told me a little red light would go on if anything serious was wrong."

"You ought to get it looked at. Preventive medicine."

"Last time I had it looked at, it cost me a hundred bucks, and it didn't run any better." The wheezing stopped. "I thought we'd go to Joe's Place. Is that okay with you? It's a tavern near where you're parked."

"You're the expert. I'm just a stranger in town."

She pulled into a parking spot as another van drew out. "I guess they'll let you in wearing a tie," she said, laughing. "This place isn't exactly the Ritz, but they serve hot pretzels free with the beer. I know all the bargains in town."

The tavern was dim and noisy, with music pounding loudly from the jukebox. The customers were young people, relaxing after work. Most of them were dressed casually. This wasn't where the office workers met. Conversation was difficult over the loud talk and music, but the beer was ice-cold and more than welcome. The pretzels were fresh and crisp. They ate the whole bowl.

"Now I'm ready for that postponed bubble bath," Sam said, gathering up her purse.

She thought Jacob might suggest they do something that night—not an expensive date, of course, but maybe a drive or just meet at his place. Since he didn't even have chairs, it occurred to her that she could invite him over to watch TV or a video.

She was just about to suggest it when he said, "I'd better be getting home. I want to do some refining on that new software for the condo. Ned Reilly had a few useful suggestions. He wants to keep track of some details that don't involve the residents, as well. Schedules on maintenance for the heating and hydro and pool."

"I'll probably just kick back and watch some TV," Sam said, to let him know she'd be home, if he felt like calling later.

They went out to her van. "I'll drive you over to pick up your car," she said.

"That's all right. I can walk. It's not far."

"It's no trouble. I have to go that way. My apartment's nearby."

"If you're sure," he said, and opened the door for her before getting in himself.

When she turned the key, the motor was dead.

"I must be out of gas," she said. "No, I can't be. I filled it up two days ago."

"Check the gauge," he said, and peered at it. The gauge registered more than half-full.

"Would it be the carburetor?" she asked uncertainly.

"This model doesn't have a carburetor. It's fuel injection. Looks like the module's gone on you."

"Darn it. Will it be expensive to get it fixed?"

"It ain't cheap," he said. "But maybe I'm wrong. Let's call a garage."

She reached for the cellular phone. Jacob was surprised she had this expensive gadget, but as she spent a lot of time on the road, it was hardly an extravagance.

She talked to the mechanic for a minute, then hung up. "He can't come for an hour. He says he'll tow it to the garage. I told him where it is. He knows my van."

"I'll drive you home."

"No, that's all right, Jake. I have to do a few errands downtown, anyway. I'll stay here and come back in an hour."

"Are you sure?"

"I'm sure, thanks."

Jacob didn't like to leave her stranded. He realized, too, that being without a car would make it impossible for her to do her job.

"Listen, Sam, if they can't get your car fixed by tomorrow, you're welcome to borrow mine. I don't use it that much."

She shook her head. "I couldn't do that to your nice car. It's practically new, and God only knows what I'd be hauling in it. The garage will give me a loaner. But thanks, anyway."

She was sure Jacob's sigh was one of relief. It was really sweet of him to make the offer. She knew what that car meant to him. Jacob left, and Sam went into the department store to pick up some shampoo and a few things she needed. She spent the rest of the hour perusing the store for new merchandise. It was part of her job, to know what the stores had available.

When the hour was up, she returned to her van and drove in the truck with the man who towed it to the garage. She waited with bated breath to hear the verdict while the mechanic did the diagnostic test.

"Your fuel injection module's gone, lady," the mechanic said with a smile that told her she was looking at an expensive repair job.

"How much?" she asked fearfully.

"Around five hundred, give or take fifty."

"Good Lord! That much!"

"Afraid so. You can shop around if you like. You won't get a better price."

"Do you take credit cards?"

"Do monkeys take peanuts?"

"Okay, go ahead. When'll it be ready?"

"For you, I'll have it done by noon tomorrow."

"Can you let me have a loaner?"

He pointed to a rusty heap in the corner. "Treat her gentle," he said, and got a set of keys from a hook on the wall.

Of course the heap was running on empty, so she had to stop and buy some gas before she went home. She emptied half the cold bathwater and topped it off with hot water, poured in a lavish amount of bubble bath and let her body sink into the soothing water. She leaned back, closed her eyes and began to do her mental arithmetic.

Rent wasn't due for two weeks. She had three hundred in her checking account, which she had planned to put toward her credit card debt, which was getting a little out of hand. The interest really added up. Oh darn, she had written a check for a hundred and fifty for the tennis club. She was sorry she'd bought the black lace dress. She certainly didn't need it. If she didn't buy anything except food and gas for a couple of weeks, she'd be all right.

When the bubbles began to disappear, she whirled her hands around in the water to reactivate them. The apple blossom bath oil smelled lovely, like a real apple orchard. It should! She'd paid ten bucks for it—but it came in a beautiful cut glass bottle that she planned to refill with cheaper bubble bath oil. When the water grew cool, she drained the tub and had a quick shower.

After a hard day's work, Sam often went out for dinner, not to a fancy restaurant, but just for a slice of pizza or a hamburger. Since she was trying to cut back on expenses, she decided to eat at home that night. She put on her terry cloth wrapper and padded to the kitchen to root for dinner.

The bowl of fruit on the counter was rapidly spoiling. She'd bought too many grapes—and they were expensive, too. She also had to throw out a couple of apples. The fridge was another tale of waste. The cheddar cheese had blue mold all over one side, and the remains of the barbecue chicken she'd bought a week ago smelled funny. Why did she buy a whole chicken? She should have bought just a bunch of wings. A half loaf of bread had also gone moldy on her.

After she had made her dinner of soup and crackers she decided to clean up the fridge and cupboards. At the back of the top cupboard shelf, she found two tins of oysters and other expensive party foods she'd forgotten all about. That was a habit she'd brought from home. Her dad always kept this kind of stuff on hand, but it made sense for him. He used it. Her friends preferred to send out for pizza or Chinese. She really had to cut back on these dumb, expensive purchases.

Sam tidied up the kitchen after eating and went into her bedroom, where more extravagant waste confronted her. She had over sixty pairs of earrings on a shelf. Magazines that she hadn't read yet stared accusingly from the bookshelf. Her closet was so full the dresses were jammed together. On her dresser, half a dozen expensive bottles of perfume were gathering dust. The bathroom was worse—how many lipsticks had she brought home, only to be dissatisfied with the color after she tried them?

Lord, she was as bad as Rue Sanderson! Well, relatively speaking. Her creams didn't cost fifty dollars an ounce, but they weren't cheap, either. If she could have back all the money she'd spent on useless junk, she could pay for her van repair in cash. She was going to turn over a new leaf, starting right now. No more monthly trims from Antonio for one thing.

At nine-thirty the phone rang. It was Ginnie Moore, Sam's old high school friend, announcing a party.

"My cousin Lorraine's coming from California. I'm getting a bunch of people together at my place. Bring a friend—preferably a gorgeous hunk."

Jacob Foster immediately popped into Sam's mind. "I might just do that," she said. "What time?"

"Eightish. Wear something fancy. Lorraine's a model. We have to uphold the honor of Findley Falls."

They talked for a quarter of an hour about the party, discussing what they'd wear and what Lorraine would probably wear, and how they'd feel like unattractive lumps beside the California beauty.

Sam was just about to phone Jacob and invite him to go with her when the phone rang.

"Hi, Sam. It's Jacob. I just called to see if you got home all right," he said.

"I made it, but my van's still there. It's going to cost five hundred dollars!" she said. "I'm still staggering under the shock of the bad news. My poor credit card'll go up in smoke. I'm pushing the limit on it as it is."

Jacob scowled. He knew Sam was having trouble making ends meet, now this. "Gee, I'm sorry, Sam. Did they give you a loaner?"

"Yes, that's covered at least. I just hope business is good. I've got to save up for my rent."

"If my deal with the condo comes off, I might be able to help you. You deserve a commission, anyway. You put me on to it."

"I'll be all right. I'm going to curtail my spending severely."

A smile of sympathy moved Jacob's lips. He figured Sam was living pretty close to the bone already. What did she plan to do, quit eating?

"If there's anything I can do to help, give me a buzz. That isn't just a nominal offer, Sam. I mean it. If you have any heavy stuff you have to move, or any customer like Mrs. Lavin who could use a strong back or some technical help, I'd be more than happy to do it. I wish I could offer you a loan, but—"

"Good heavens, Jacob, I wouldn't accept a loan from a new acquaintance! But thanks for offering. I appreciate it. I was just going to call you, by the way. If you're free tomorrow night, a friend of mine is having a party. Her cousin's visiting from L.A. We could really use a New Yorker to lend us a touch of class."

He laughed modestly. "I don't consider myself a New Yorker, but I'd be happy to come."

"Great, Ginnie said eightish. If you call for me at eight, we'll have a drink and be there before nine. We wouldn't want to be the first ones there."

"Is this a suit and tie party, or a jeans and sneakers party?"

"Shirt and tie, and my best bib and tucker for me."

"That'll be nice. I've never seen you dressed up."

He sounded curious. Sam decided she'd wear something really sensational, to show him her wardrobe did hold something other than jeans.

"Then you ain't seen nothing yet," she joked. "How's the program going?"

"Oh, that's all done. I'm working on our video game now."

"The marrying game or the shopping game?"

"The marrying game."

"Give mechanics zero points," she said, then paused. "Or maybe a hundred, like you and Einstein. They must be loaded, at the prices they charge."

"Surely money isn't the only criterion?" he asked.

"No, but it's right up there when you're as broke as I am."

"Make that as broke as we are."

He talked for a long time, explaining that he had given each profession in the computer game an actual name. Doctor Sawbones, Dentist Driller, Professor Dimwit, Author Readwell, Artist Splatter and so on.

"And Mechanic Rip-Off," she suggested.

"That's hardly fair. You're just sore because your van broke down. We'll call the mechanic Mr. Wrench."

"Good choice. That's what he gave my wallet all right."

When she hung up, Sam felt better about life in general. So her van broke down—big deal. The repairs were deductible—the cost of doing business. Her business was doing well, and now she had an interesting man in her life. A really thoughtful, generous man, who offered to help when she was in a pinch. None of the people she referred to as her friends had ever offered her their cars when hers was out of commission or offered to help her with any heavy job that came along. Jacob Foster seemed the kind of man she could get serious about.

Chapter Four

Most workers got the weekend off, but Saturday was Sam's busiest day. With the gardening season getting under way, she had a few trips to the gardening centers and one order to buy a lawn mower. She went to the gardening center and made her selections in the morning, to be picked up in the afternoon when she got her van back. The lawn mower fitted in the back of the loaner, and she delivered it in the morning.

She also had a few flat-rate jobs, one to exchange a pair of shoes for a bride whose feet had apparently swollen since she'd bought her shoes. She couldn't get into them. The store didn't have the ones she'd chosen in the larger size, so Sam took a couple of pairs to the bride's house for her to choose from.

Another bride... How did all these other women find a man they could love enough to marry? Was she too choosy? This was often discussed between Ginnie and herself. They had agreed in high school that they'd hold out for true love; nothing had changed their minds about that.

Sam had an arrangement with a senior citizens' home to pick up their monthly supply of liquor. This sounded racy, but in fact consisted of one bottle a month for those who drank; usually it was sherry. The store would probably have delivered it for them, but Sam had got the seniors a special on a TV and VCR. She also had a very special flat rate for their small purchases. She often picked up videos for them gratis, and they were faithful to their friends. She felt a special closeness to them. They reminded her of her grandparents, who had been so kind to her years ago.

At five o'clock she was home, pleasantly tired and ready for a party. She made tuna salad for dinner, sticking to her rule of eating cheap, without being unhealthy. She showered, washed her hair and dried it with the blow dryer to give it some lift, the way Antonio had showed her. It gleamed like a new penny, the copper color in contrast to her ivory skin. Like everyone else, she was staying out of the sun that year to protect her skin. She brushed a little rouge high on her cheekbones, applied lipstick, saving her eye makeup for last.

She wanted to look sleek and sophisticated, to show Jacob there was more to Sam Sherman than jeans and sneakers. She outlined her eyes subtly in kohl, drew mascara through her lashes, and brushed a silvery gray eye shadow on her lids. Amazing how a little makeup could turn a tomboy into a glamorous woman. The dangling jade earrings completed the effect. They also emphasized the cat green of her eyes.

When she was all made up, she slid the black lace dress over her head. The flappers had worn their dresses loose. Sam figured the flapper who owned this one must have been smaller than she. It fit her like a glove, clinging to her breasts and hugging her body. It hung just above the knees, giving it a modern look. The incongruity of her boyish hairdo enhanced the femininity of the dress. Maybe Antonio was worth the price after all.

At a quarter to eight she was just checking the fridge to see what she had in the way of drinks when the phone rang.

"Sam, it's Rue," the familiar voice said. "Help! Emergency! I'm out of vodka again, and the colonel is coming over for drinks. He won't touch anything except vodka martinis. Darling, would you mind terribly...?" Just like her mom! How often had her mother sent her off in a great rush to buy something when company was coming? At times Sam felt she was the mother of the house. Her mom also used to call her "darling."

Rue usually ran out of vodka at least once a month, usually when the liquor stores were closed. Sam had acquired the habit of keeping a bottle on hand herself, to avoid scrambling all over town.

"I'm expecting company in fifteen minutes," Sam said. "We'll drop it off on our way to our party. Is that okay?"

"Darling, the colonel is on his way up *now!* Couldn't you bring it right over? I know I'm a terrible pest. How do you put up with me?"

"It's no problem, Rue. I'll call Jacob and see if he's left yet. He could meet me at your place."

"You're an angel! Jacob—is that the man Annie Lavin was telling me about? She said he's wildly handsome. Something to do with lamps..."

"That's the one, but he works with computer software, not lamps."

"Darling, bring him up for a drink. I'd love to meet him. I want to see what kind of men you're going out with, see if he's good enough for you."

"I'll ask him to come." Sam smiled softly. Yeah, definitely Rue was her mother substitute. She actually felt a twinge of apprehension, wondering if Rue would like Jacob. Well, she was sure her mom would have liked him, so Rue probably would, too. Those helpless women liked a take-charge kind of man.

Sam caught Jacob just as he was leaving and explained the situation. "Would you mind meeting me at the Regency Tower? Rue's a very good customer. I don't like to let her down."

Jacob was annoyed for Sam. Personally, he didn't mind going to the Regency Tower to pick her up, but he disliked that those women were using her. "No problem," he said. "What's her last name?"

"Sanderson, the penthouse. Thanks a heap, Jacob."

She got out the vodka and decided to walk around the corner to Rue's apartment. It was just as fast as having to park the van, and she'd have to drive it home later, since Jacob was picking her up in his car.

Rue was waiting for her. "You're a lifesaver," she said, giving Sam a hug and a kiss on the cheek. She handed Sam the money for the vodka plus a tip. "Come on in and say hello to Colonel Walker. You remember the colonel."

Sam had met the colonel a few times at Rue's place. He was a retired officer with a walrus mustache and a sergeant major's strong voice. He managed to lend a military air to a seersucker suit and loafers.

Rue made the martinis and poured Sam's favorite white wine. "Don't you look nice!" she complimented. "I never imagined you in black, Sam. So sophisticated. Really it's only the young who can wear black."

When the doorbell sounded, Sam said, "That must be Jacob. I'll get it."

She opened the door and said, "Hi, you found it. Come on in."

Jacob just stood there, as if he had been hit with a stun gun. "Is that *you?*" he asked. Where had this glamorous woman come from? She looked as if she'd stepped out of the pages of a fashion magazine. If it weren't for the red hair, he could have thought he'd come to the wrong address. This woman looked as if she belonged in the ritzy Regency Tower.

"This old thing?" She laughed. "It's the dress I got at the thrift shop. I told you I had a new dress. It's real vintage lace. Do you like it?" She turned around to show off the dress.

"Very much." Her down-to-earth conversation reassured him that he hadn't wandered into a dream. He studied her closely. It was just the makeup and those earrings that had changed her so.

"You look nice, too, Jacob. Come on in and meet Rue."

He followed her into the most lavish apartment he'd ever seen, outside of his boss's place in New York. His boss's had been an imitation English gentlemen's club. This one looked like the set of a Fred Astaire movie. "I feel like I should dance in," he murmured.

"I know what you mean. It's called Art Deco, if you want to compliment Rue."

"Mrs. Sanderson." Jacob smiled when Sam introduced them. He shook her hand formally. "What a lovely apartment."

"Oh, do you like it?" Before he had time to drop the words *Art Deco*, she continued chatting. "Please call me Rue. And I'll call you Jacob. We're all friends here. You're the computer expert Annie Lavin is raving about." She put her hand on Jacob's arm to lead him in. Over her shoulder, she gave Sam a big smile. Rue liked him! Sam was sure she would. Rue introduced him to Colonel Walker.

"Computers, eh?" the colonel said. "Could've used them in the war, I daresay. Not on the field of battle, but at HQ. That's the Second World War I'm talking about." Jacob expressed interest, and the colonel continued. "I was at Iwo Jima—of course I was a youngster in those days."

"You were a marine!" Jacob exclaimed.

Colonel Walker's mustache twitched in pleasure. "Ah, you are aware of such things. It's surprising to find a youngster nowadays who remembers. One sometimes thinks it was all a dream—or a nightmare."

"It must have been horrendous," Jacob said. "I've never met anyone who was actually there. Would it be too harrowing for you to tell me a little about it?"

The colonel was not slow to oblige him.

Rue said, "We'll leave you gentlemen to your war talk. I have a little business to discuss with Sam." Sam was sorry she had to miss the colonel's war stories.

"About Paris," Rue began. "I've made up a list of things I'll need." She went over the list in great detail while the colonel and Jake talked. Actually Jacob asked an occasional question, and the colonel talked.

Rue said, "I'd like to leave my apartment key with you, Sam, and maybe you could pop in a couple of times a week to check my phone messages. I'll leave you my Paris number. You can call from here, so the calls will be on my bill. I like to keep in touch with my friends while I'm away. Oh, and the mail! I'm expecting an invitation from Marj Spencer to her daughter's wedding. I'd like you to open it when it arrives and give me the date. I don't want to miss that."

Another wedding! It seemed to Sam that her whole generation was getting married. She jotted down that and a few other items in her notepad. "Anything else?" she asked.

"Yes, there's one other thing. I want someone to keep Beckie for me." Beckie was her Lhasa apso. She was a noisy, troublesome small dog that Rue usually kept locked in the kitchen when company came, since the dog couldn't behave herself.

"What about the kennel where you usually leave her?" Sam asked.

"She hates the kennel. I was wondering if you—"

"I'm sorry, my apartment building doesn't allow dogs. I could visit Beckie at the kennel, maybe take her for walks or something."

Rue sighed. "That'd be better than nothing, but she really does hate that kennel. She lost a pound last time. That's a lot of weight for a little Lhasa apso."

"I don't know what to suggest. Most apartments don't allow dogs. You need someone with a house."

The men had come to a pause in their conversation. "Did you say something about a dog needing a house?" Jacob asked. "I'm renting a house. I love dogs."

Rue beamed a thousand-watt smile at him. "Would you? I know I can trust any friend of Sam's. I'll let you meet Beckie. I have to lock her up when company comes. She's so sociable. She just loves people."

Sam knew *sociable* was a euphemism for *untrained*. The little dog jumped all over people. Jacob didn't seem to mind, however. In fact, he seemed as pleased as a kid with his first pet. He made a fuss over Beckie, who licked his hand in friendly response. "She'll be good company for me," he said, stroking Beckie into silence.

Rue gave him an assessing look. "I wouldn't think you'd have much trouble finding company, Jacob." Jacob didn't blush, but he looked embarrassed. Rue laughed. "Sam will drop in from time to time." She looked at Sam for agreement.

"I'll make sure they're getting along," she agreed.

"You know my vet and all that sort of thing, Sam. I'll send a case of Beckie's food over with her. She won't be any trouble. I'm leaving Monday afternoon. Where do you live, Jacob?"

"On Alberry Drive, but I'll be happy to pick up Beckie. I'll be dropping in to visit Ned Reilly Monday morning."

"Oh yes, about the computer," Rue said. "I'm in favor of it. I'll leave my proxy vote with Annie Lavin."

Sam and Jacob soon left. "Rue liked you. Very sly, offering to mind Beckie," Sam said with a teasing look.

"No, I really do like dogs. You don't think that's why I did it?" He looked offended.

"That may not be why you did it, but it sure won't do you any harm. You seemed to hit it off pretty well with the colonel, too. Unfortunately he doesn't have a vote. He lives in one of the other big apartment buildings in town."

"He has some wicked stories," Jacob said. "He was at Bloody Gorge."

"What's that? It sounds gruesome."

"It was one of the fiercest battles of Iwo Jima. The man's a hero. He has the Congressional Medal of Honor, for bravery in battle."

Sam had met Colonel Walker twice before, and always thought him a bore, almost a joke, with his military mannerisms. She vaguely remembered seeing a row of medals on his blazer once last winter. She realized she had been superficial. "I think he enjoyed being asked about it," she said.

"It's a shame that people forget so quickly. I just hope I didn't call up too many unpleasant memories for him—and at a party, too. It was thoughtless of me."

"No, it wasn't thoughtless," she said. "He'll be glad to know that not everyone has forgotten." Forgotten? She didn't know the first thing about Iwo Jima. To her, it was just that famous photograph of the soldiers—marines—raising the American flag.

They went out to Jacob's car. "I'll give you directions to Ginnie's house," she said. "You turn south at the light."

Jacob was surprised that Sam's friend lived in such an elegant part of town. The houses were set far back on large, landscaped lots. Ginnie's house looked like an antebellum mansion. Miles of white house seemed to stretch on either side of a wide veranda, with old wrought iron lamps burning. There were expensive cars parked all along the drive. Music drifted out from the house.

"How'd you meet this Ginnie?" he asked. "Did you do some shopping for her? She must be a millionaire."

"I've known her for ages. I went to school in Findley Falls for a couple of years when my mom died. I stayed with my grandparents. They're both dead now."

Jacob made some sympathetic noises. It must have been hard on Sam, her mother dying when she was so young, moving to another town. Maybe that was what made her so independent.

Sam just gave the doorbell one ring and walked in. Ginnie came to welcome her. She was tall, slender and dark haired. What Jacob instinctively thought of as a 'lady.' There was a subtle air of breeding about her. He was a little surprised that she and Sam were apparently good friends.

Sam introduced Ginnie and Jacob. She saw at once that Ginnie was favorably impressed.

"Come on in and meet everybody. They're dancing in the rec room," she said. Over her shoulder to Sam she whispered. "Where'd you get him? He's gorgeous!"

"You said to bring a handsome hunk," Sam replied in her usual voice. Jacob looked at her, embarrassed but flattered. Sam winked playfully.

Two dozen guests were dancing in a long room with a black and white tiled floor. Ginnie introduced them to a few people who hadn't started dancing yet, including her cousin, Lorraine. She was a long-legged, long-haired blonde with more style than beauty.

"The bar's to your right. Help yourself," Ginnie said.

"Want a drink, or do you want to dance?" Sam asked Jacob.

"We've just had a drink. Let's dance. Unless you—"

"We'll work up a thirst first."

They danced for half an hour. Jacob was a good dancer; Sam was better than good. She threw her whole energy into it, the same as she did with everything else. As her slender body moved in time with the music, the lights flickered from her hair. Jacob felt he was with the prettiest woman in the room.

"I forgot to ask you if you got your van back," he said, when the music stopped. "You looked so glamorous you put it right out of my mind."

"I got it back, and thanks for the compliment. Let's have that drink now. Are you thirsty?"

"I could do with a beer."

They took two bottles out to the garden to sit in lounge chairs, looking at the long stretch of yard, edged with an herbaceous border. A sweet smell of newly mown grass and earth and flowers hung on the air. A lopsided moon flooded the garden with half light, giving it a ghostly aspect.

They sipped their drinks, while cooling off from the exercise of dancing. "I'm looking forward to minding Beckie," Jacob said in a nostalgic tone.

"Minding her is right. She hasn't been well trained. Make sure you lock up your shoes, and don't let her near your office. She'll make papier-mâché of your printouts."

"I'll take her for long walks. That'll get rid of her frustrations. Maybe you'll come with us sometimes?"

"Sure, I promised Rue I'd drop in. Make sure you get her leash."

They chatted idly until their glasses were empty. "Do you want to go back in and dance?" Jacob asked.

Sam thought she heard a note of reluctance in his voice. When she looked up at the romantic moon and around at the garden, she felt some reluctance to leave herself.

"It's so nice out here. Let's take a stroll. There's a gazebo at the back of the garden. Ginnie and I used to study for our exams out there when we were in high school. Mostly we talked about boys," she said. "We were both madly in love with the team's quarterback. You would have hated us. We were like those girls you had to beat off with a club in college."

Jacob was amused by her frankness. "You were the one who said that. As a matter of fact, I did play quarterback, though. But I'm not carrying a club," he added, tilting his head down to peer at her.

"And I'm no longer a teenager."

They strolled hand in hand past the flowering bushes. The roses weren't in bloom yet, but something was giving off a lovely perfume. The white gazebo looked like a skeletal house in the shadows. Wrought iron Victorian curlicues curved around the door and roof. Vines grew up the side of the posts that formed an open wall. They went up the two steps into the dark privacy of the little open house.

"I haven't been in here for years," Sam said, remembering the long talks with Ginnie in the old days, when every new boyfriend, every movie and every new sweater had to be discussed at length. "It makes me feel like a teenager again."

"What are you, all of twenty-two or three?"

Her chin came up pugnaciously. "I'm twenty-four."

"That old!" he joked. "I guess that makes me Methuselah. I'll never see my twenties again. Turned thirty last month." He shook his head. "Thirty years old, and I don't have a wife or kids, a house or even a job. My dad had Mom and me and my sister when he was my age."

"I didn't know you had a sister. How come you never mentioned her?"

"Beth's married, she lives in Denver now. I don't get to see her as often as I'd like to. She named her first-born after me."

"That's nice. She must like you."

"She does, but I'm not so sure Jacobina will appreciate having my name."

"Oh, she was a girl!" she said, and laughed. "Boy, your sister must really like you, to subject her daughter to that."

"She does." Jacob turned and studied her shadowed face. "So far you've said Mrs. Lavin likes me, Ginnie likes me, Rue likes me, my sister likes me. I seem to be liked by everyone except you."

A smile glinted up at him. Shafts of moonlight creeping through the vine bathed her face in a pale glow. Her eyes looked like silver—no, diamonds. They sparkled.

"I like you, too," she said simply. "You're a nice man, Jacob."

Jacob felt a glow of pleasure. He answered in the same blunt way. "I like you, too, Sam."

"Good! Now that the mutual admiration society has made its verdict, shall we go back to the party?"

"What's your hurry? The best parties consist of two people." He took her hand and squeezed it. "I think it's important to like the person you love, don't you?"

She looked confused. "I don't know what you mean. Naturally you like a person you love. Like comes first, then love."

"That hasn't been my experience," he said. "Love— or to call it by its right name, lust—can be experienced without really liking a person."

Sam thought Jacob had had that experience, and felt a sting of something sharp. It took her a moment to realize it was jealousy. "Was this a recent experience?" she asked in an offhand way.

"Fairly recent. I was going out with a woman from the office in New York. A very intelligent, pretty woman. A programmer, like myself. I thought we were in love, or falling in love, at least. It turned out she thought I could protect her from being laid off. I was the most senior employee, other than the partners who owned the place. When they let her go, she was furious with me. She wouldn't see me, wouldn't even speak to me on the phone. I was no longer of use to her. Boy, was I stupid!"

"It's better you found out what she was like before you did something really stupid, like marry her," Sam said, and knew it was just the trite sort of reply anyone would make. Strangely, she felt no sympathy at all, but only a sense of annoyance.

"Yeah, that's why I think it's important to really know someone, and like her, before falling in love with her." He looked down and smiled. "I like you, Sam," he said again.

Sam didn't say anything, but she felt as though she had received a great compliment. She just looked at him for a long moment. He took it as an invitation, or at least permission, to kiss her. The same chemistry she had felt the first time he kissed her was still there, enhanced this time by the romantic surroundings. They were alone, in this leafy glade, with the moonlight dancing over them, surrounded by the sweet smells of springtime.

Jacob's kiss seemed as elemental as the surroundings. It wasn't just that superficial lust he had mentioned, although that was there, too, quickening her pulse and causing the blood to race in her veins. The feeling went right to her vital core. She knew she was being kissed by a man who truly cared for her, a man she could trust.

His chest was strong and warm as his arms folded protectively around her. They tightened to a vise as the kiss deepened to passion. A moist flicker at her lips sent a quiver of anticipation rippling down her spine. She opened her lips, and felt the warm intimacy of his tongue mating with hers. One hand was at her nape, his fingers moving with a gentle fever, encouragingly.

She lifted one arm and ran her fingers through his silky hair, which curled at his collar. When she let her fingers play over his cheek, she heard a soft moan of approval echo from deep in his throat. The tension was building fast, too fast. She didn't really know Jacob that well. They'd only been acquainted for a couple of days. When his hand moved under the top of her dress, she pulled reluctantly away.

"I like you, and the chemistry ain't bad, either," she said frankly, "but I think it's a little early to call it love, don't you?"

An impish grin flashed. "Maybe, a little. It's only ten o'clock. We'll try again around midnight, or whenever the party's over."

They walked slowly, arm in arm, back to the party and danced with each other and with a few other people. Since Lorraine didn't know anyone, all the men had a dance with her. Whoever Sam and Jacob danced with, their minds were on each other. Their eyes would meet across the room and hold. Those looks held a promise of intimacy to come.

At midnight, Ginnie served chili, followed by a big cake with a message welcoming Lorraine to Findley Falls. There was more dancing after, but when Jacob suggested they leave, Sam agreed. She was a little nervous about his suggestion that they'd 'try again.' What did he mean, exactly? She had no intention of going to bed with him. It was reassuring to know he wasn't the kind of man who would persist. She felt she knew him well enough to be sure of that, so she invited him up for coffee.

"That sounds good," Jacob said. "I don't know exactly where you live. Somewhere near Rue's place, isn't it?"

"Just around the corner and down half a block."

Since Rue's condo was on a very fancy street, Jacob assumed the real estate took a rapid decline when you turned the corner. He was surprised to see another glass and steel building, not very different from Rue's.

"Right there," she said, pointing to it.

"You live there!" he exclaimed.

"I just rent. I don't own the apartment, like Rue."

"The rent must be pretty steep," he said. It immediately popped into his head that poor Sam was out of her depth. She had gotten involved in one of those deals where you got a couple of months rent free, but would she ever be able to keep up the monthly payments?

"Actually my dad chose the place," she said, and felt childish to admit it.

"Does he know what you do for a living?"

"Of course he knows. He bought my van for me and paid the first and last month's rent on my apartment." She figured she might as well confess the whole thing while she was at it.

Jacob just stared at her. "Is he rich?" he asked in a surprised tone.

She shrugged. "Small town rich. He doesn't own a string of racing horses or a chalet in Switzerland. He's a lawyer."

Jacob was confused. He kept hearing the States had an abundant supply of lawyers. A lawyer could be anything from a man struggling to make a living to a millionaire. He didn't think Mr. Sherman was struggling too hard if he had given his daughter a van and moved her into this fancy address.

"What kind of lawyer?" he asked.

"A corporate lawyer."

As Jacob had already asked more questions that he had any right to, he let it drop.

The lobby was about what Jacob expected—a sea of marble, lots of plants and mirrors. At least the elevator stopped at floor fourteen, before they got to the penthouse. The hallway wasn't carpeted, but the terrazzo floor gleamed like new. Sam stopped at apartment nine and went in before him to switch on the lights.

If it had been anyone else's apartment, Jacob would have loved it. The light reflecting from the peach walls bathed the living room in a warm golden glow, with glass and brass twinkling discreetly. He looked around slowly, noticing the handsome white leather sofa, the thick carpeting and the modern prints and painting on the walls. It looked like something out of a movie or a decorating magazine. He felt cheated. Here he had been feeling sorry for Sam, and all the time she was a spoiled rich kid.

"Nice place," he said hollowly.

"Thanks, I did the decorating myself. The place is small but cozy. Now, how about that coffee?"

He noticed Sam had kicked off her shoes. He hadn't seen her do it, but he suddenly felt he should have done the same before treading on the fancy carpet. "Fine," he said. "Can I help?"

"Why don't you just put on some music and kick back? I won't be a minute." Sam disappeared down the corridor.

Jacob turned on the radio—an expensive one. He noticed Sam also had good stereo equipment, stacks of tapes, a CD. He sat on the edge of the sofa and continued examining the room. The coffee table held a selection of the latest magazines, mostly fashion and decorating, with a couple of light news weeklies. A heavy glass bowl held pistachio nuts. The lamps weren't white marble, but they looked as if they might have come from that shop with the snooty clerk.

All the small appointments of the room were expensive and, he had to admit, lovely. He'd seen that reproduction of Degas's young ballerina statue for sale in a museum shop, and had nearly bought one—in the old days, when he had plenty of money. The prints on the wall were by famous artists, a Chagall and a Picasso. He went for a closer look at the one original oil painting, and saw it signed Lou Natique. Never heard of him anyway. He was afraid it'd be van Gogh. It wouldn't have surprised him much at that point.

Why the devil was Sam doing such hard, menial work, when she was obviously as rich as Croesus? Why was she buying secondhand clothes and worrying about her van breaking down? Surely her dad would be glad to bail her out. Here he'd been feeling sorry for her, thinking she was a working girl. She was probably laughing at him the whole time.

She soon appeared with the coffee and a plate of thin, chocolate-covered cookies, the expensive kind that came in tins. The cups were delicate china, not the mugs he would have expected earlier.

He watched as she poured the steaming coffee into the cups. Looking at her from a new perspective, he noticed how elegantly she moved, her wrist arched daintily, like a well-reared young lady. Her black lace dress just suited the role. That's what she did, she played roles, from struggling worker in jeans to society woman in black lace. Sam smiled politely as she offered the cookies.

"Try one of these. They're from Belgium and are delicious." Jacob took one and had to agree it was delicious, but it might as well have been ashes.

"It was a nice party, wasn't it?" Sam said, to get the conversational ball rolling.

"Yeah, sure was."

"And it's nice getting home, too." She rearranged herself on the sofa, pulling her shoeless feet under her.

"I like the way you've decorated your place," he said, as it was his turn to say something. Natural conversation seemed to have dried up.

"I'd be glad to help you do yours, when you're ready."

"I couldn't afford anything like this." He gestured around the room with a sweep of his arm.

"It didn't cost much. I'm a professional shopper, remember? I know where to get bargains."

"Including original oil paintings?"

"You mean my Lou Natique?" She laughed. "That's a joke, Jacob. Lunatic—get it? It was done by a friend of mine at college. He gave it to me for my birthday, since he couldn't afford to buy me a present. I couldn't afford a Lou Natique now. Lou's selling for thousands. His real name's Lou Nader. Have you heard of him?"

"No, I don't tour the galleries much." He gave her a disillusioned look. "Why do you bother with that job of yours, Sam?"

Sam always felt a sting of annoyance when people put down her job. "I told you, I like it. It's fun."

"That's right. You did."

That was probably the only reason she did it. She liked it. It was fun—until she got bored with it and took up something else...decorating or fashion design. Sam was fun, he admitted, but he'd had enough of fun women who dropped you when they wanted a new kind of entertainment or when you were of no further use to them.

At least he could acquit Sam of using him for personal gain. What could he do for a woman like her? Amuse her, for a while. And what could she do for him? Just waste his time and maybe break his heart.

He drank up his coffee quickly. Sam was still a little nervous about that "we'll try again." She picked up the coffeepot to refill his cup.

"One's enough for me," he said.

"I made a whole pot of coffee. It's decaf, so you don't have to worry it'll keep you awake."

"I'd better be going."

"Going!" Here she thought he was going to make his move. "You just got here!"

He gazed at her across the short length of the love seat. "I don't think this relationship is going anywhere, Sam. Let's just chalk it up to experience."

"But you said you liked me!" she blurted out, without thinking.

"I do. We'll be friends, okay?"

Sam set her cup down and stared at him. "Let's have it, Jacob. What's the matter? I thought the coffee was pretty good, myself," she added lightly.

His eyes made a silent tour of the room. Every expensive lamp and picture seemed to be mocking him, as he mentally compared his hovel to this. And he had felt sorry for her! Boy, talk about a dope. "I thought you were a poor, struggling worker, like me."

"I am!"

"If you really believe you're poor, you must be even richer than I thought. Or at least your dad must be."

"Yes, as a matter of fact, he does pretty well for himself, but I hardly have a penny to my name."

"You could always hock your diamonds."

"I don't have any diamonds."

"I'm sure you will, one day." That was the kind of guy she'd marry. Some man who'd shower her with diamonds and yachts. What did he have to offer? An unfurnished, rented little house in a second-rate suburban development.

"Actually, I'm not into diamonds."

He smiled sardonically. "Hold out for emeralds—to match your eyes."

Then he stood up to leave. "It was a nice party, Sam. Thanks for asking me."

"Good night, Jake," she said in a cold voice. "See you around." He left.

If he was going to be like that, she'd call him Jake from now on, and to hell with him. How dare he criticize the way she lived? She had a pretty good idea what this snit was all about. He was just mad because she had a nice apartment, and a rich father. He didn't say it—he didn't have to. She knew he thought she was spoiled. She worked her buns off, taking flak from all her customers. She worked just as hard as he did, and if he thought she should apologize for being able to have nice things, he could go fly a kite.

Where had she got the idea he was a nice man? He was a narrow-minded, judgmental jerk, and if he thought she wanted to continue being friends with someone like that, he was crazy. She picked up a cookie and bit into it. She'd better enjoy it, because this was the bottom of the box of Belgian biscuits, and there wouldn't be any more of them under the new austerity regime. She couldn't even afford a box of her favorite cookies, and Jake had the nerve to imply she was spoiled!

She punched the cushions and carried the tray out to the kitchen. To hell with Jake Foster.

Chapter Five

Sam didn't expect Jake to call, and he didn't. When Ginnie invited her and Jake to make up a fourth for tennis with Lorraine the next afternoon, Sam said, "I believe Jake has other plans, but I'd like to play."

"I hope you're not going to let that gorgeous hunk escape," Ginnie said.

"We're just friends," Sam replied. The words called up a memory of last night, when Jake had suddenly turned into an icicle before her very eyes. Who wanted to be friends with an icicle?

"Sounds like a lovers' quarrel to me," Ginnie said.

"We're not lovers, and it wasn't exactly a quarrel, but I can't invite him to play tennis. Don't ask."

After a slight pause Ginnie said, "Is he officially available then? I mean you said you and he were just friends. I don't want to intrude, but if it isn't a romance..."

"Give it your best shot, but I doubt you'll get any farther than I did."

"Why, what's wrong with him?" Ginnie asked suspiciously.

"He doesn't like us spoiled little rich girls."

"Spoiled? I'm a hardworking nurse. And you're not exactly on easy street yourself."

"It's kind of complicated. Jake's between jobs at the moment."

"I see. That's tough on a man's ego. All prickly and uptight, huh?"

"I guess you could say that. What time's the tennis game?"

"I have a court booked for one-thirty. I'll call Nancy to make up a fourth." Nancy was another high school friend. "Maybe we'll luck out and meet some nice guys there."

Nancy was free and glad to fill in. She was a farmer's daughter and had a healthy, countrified look about her, despite having lived in the city for a few years. She wore her thick blond hair in a French braid, hoping to lend a touch of sophistication to her full cheeks and freckles.

Lorraine was practically a professional-class tennis player. She soon found a partner worthy of her skill and played singles with him, leaving the other three women one player short. They found an unattached male to fill in, but he disappeared as soon as the game was over. Lorraine was enjoying herself so much that they had to wait an hour until another court was available, so she could play again. They got a soft drink and waited in the shade, watching Lorraine and talking desultorily about life. Sam ignored all her friends' hints to talk about Jake.

"Sorry, I'm not in a mood to say anything good about him, so I won't say anything."

Nancy Ryder was in a glum mood. She'd been laid off herself and would have to return home to live on her parents' farm outside of town if she didn't find a job soon. She had been secretary to the chief engineer at a local factory that had recently closed down.

"I really hate to leave Findley Falls," she said. "If I could just hang on for one more month, I'm sure something would come up. I'm sorry I bought that new stereo."

"Sell it," Ginnie suggested.

"I wouldn't get half what it's worth."

Sam said, "I'm short myself, or I'd lend you the money, Nancy."

"Same here," Ginnie said. "Darned car payments are keeping me stone broke."

"What we ought to do is have a garage sale," Sam said, thinking of Nancy's stereo and all the useless items she'd bought over the years. They were just cluttering up her small apartment. "Only we'd need a garage, or at least a driveway. I couldn't do it at my apartment."

"Hey, that's not a bad idea!" Nancy grinned. She looked at Ginnie. "Like Sam said, we need a garage, or a driveway. Hint, hint. Know anybody with a garage, Ginnie?"

"All right. I can take a hint. Mom won't mind. It won't be the first garage sale on Pilton Crescent."

They discussed the logistics of it until Lorraine finished her game. She sauntered slowly toward them and said, "Luke's invited me out for a drink. Do you mind, Ginnie? You can tell Aunt Helen I'll be home for dinner."

"That's fine. You go ahead, Lorraine," Ginnie said through clenched jaws. When her cousin had left, she said, "Nice of her to let us know, after we've sat twiddling our thumbs for an hour waiting. I wonder if anyone would like to buy a slightly used cousin."

Sunday evening the women got together to discuss the garage sale. Lorraine was out with Luke. Sam was glad for an excuse to get out of her apartment, because she felt a nearly overwhelming urge to phone Jake.

The women all agreed they'd include clothing and jewelry, along with records, tapes and books in the sale. They each had some more valuable items they never used as well. Nancy had a camera she'd replaced with a better one, cross country skis, a ten-speed bicycle she didn't use and a kilim rug that didn't match anything else in her apartment. Since buying the new stereo, she was changing to tapes and wanted to unload her old records.

Sam had a typewriter that had been gathering dust since she'd gotten her word processor, a couple of unneeded lamps and small items of furniture, her old luggage that was stored in the basement locker, along with some sports equipment. Ginnie's mother had a whole garage full of discarded furniture and household goods.

"I'll put the ad in the paper," Ginnie said. "We'll have to get some signs and post them around the neighborhood. Can you do that, Nancy?"

"Sure, I have plenty of time, since I'm out of work."

"Call it a multifamily garage sale," Sam said. "It sounds bigger, and we're all from different families. We can use my van to bring our stuff over, Nancy. Get your stuff all collected up. We'll need some tables. Maybe planks of wood propped up on something."

"I'll handle that. We can use the Ping-Pong table for starters," Ginnie said. "Friday night we'll sort everything out and put the price tags on. You'd better come early on Saturday, around seven. We'll start at eight, and no early birds. We'll serve coffee and donuts."

Sam felt a wince. Even a simple thing like coffee and donuts reminded her of Jake.

"No, we'll *sell* coffee and donuts," Nancy said. "We can't afford to give them away."

"I'll borrow one of those big coffee machines from the supermarket," Sam said. "And I'll pick up the donuts. It'll be fun. And it'll be good to get all the junk cleared out of the apartment."

"Yeah, to make room for new junk." Ginnie laughed.

When she went home, Sam spent a couple of hours going through her closet and costume jewelry, setting aside the unwise purchases she'd made and regretting them. She'd only get a small fraction of what they were worth. Why on earth had she bought that purple turtleneck sweater? She could never wear a wool turtleneck. It made her neck itchy, but she loved the color.

Maybe she *was* just a *little* spoiled. She didn't take money from her dad, but she had never had to plan for her future. She knew she was the sole beneficiary of her father's will, so she felt free to spend whatever she made.

She felt restless, and eventually realized that what she was waiting for was the phone. Maybe Jake would call and apologize. Maybe he had phoned—she'd been out all day. Should she call him? No, she had her pride. Besides, tomorrow he'd be picking up Beckie. Since she'd promised Rue to keep an eye on the dog, she had a perfect excuse to call, without seeming overly eager. She didn't intend to give Jake the idea she was running after him. She knew how he felt about that!

The phone still hadn't rung when Sam went to bed. Her duvet reminded her of the pretty flowered comforter she'd used before she'd bought the duvet. That could go in the garage sale. Now where had she put it? In her old luggage in the locker, was it? She hoped it hadn't become mildewy. She forced her mind to think of items for the garage sale, to prevent thinking of Jake. Finally her eyelids fluttered closed.

In the morning, shafts of sunlight slanting in around the curtains told her it was a sunny day. She wore a T-shirt with a Windbreaker over it. If it turned hot, she could take off the outer jacket. She'd be busy running all over town for Rue, so she wore her usual jeans and comfortable sneakers. She remembered to pick up her sunglasses on her way out the door. Another extravagant purchase. Did she really need hundred-dollar sunglasses?

She got Rue's list and began her buying trip. Jacob had said he'd pick up Beckie in the morning, so Sam planned to be at the Regency Tower around ten-thirty. That seemed a likely time for him to call. But when she took Rue's purchases to her, Beckie was still there, chewing on Rue's good kid gloves and jumping all over the place.

Sam stayed for half an hour, going over the list of things to be done while Rue was away. All the time she kept listening for the sound of the buzzer announcing Jake's arrival. At eleven she left. She couldn't drag the visit out any longer. She had a living to make.

Mondays were usually slow, so she didn't worry when there were no messages. She spent the morning refurbishing the items for the garage sale. Some of the clothing had to be washed, and she tumbled the comforter in the dryer with a fabric softener to make it smell nice. It wasn't till noon that she began to look expectantly at the phone. Jake must have picked up Beckie by now. Maybe he'd call to ask for some advice.

When the phone rang at one-thirty, she dashed hopefully to answer it. It was a client wanting some cheap office furniture, like Jake. Another laid-off customer setting up shop for himself. She went around to Lou Vincent's and struck a good bargain.

Jake didn't call that evening, either. Sam drove to the airport with Ginnie to see Lorraine off. They stopped at the tennis club after and met an old school friend. Sam had gone out with Rob Staynor a few times in high school. She hardly recognized this tall, blond Adonis as the kid she'd dated all those years ago. He was working for a stockbroker in Chicago now, just home for his holidays. He asked Sam out for dinner one evening to reminisce about the old days.

"I'd love to, Rob."

"We'll go to the Napoli Garden." It was a pricey Italian restuarant. "I never could afford it when I was at school. Do you like Italian food?"

"Do cats like cream?" she returned, licking her lips. "I love it."

"Good, then I'll pick you up around eight."

When he left, Ginnie said, "It's not fair! You've got Jacob Foster, now Rob Staynor."

"I haven't got Jake."

"Well, neither have I. I called him, since you said you didn't mind. I invited him to a company dinner Dad's giving. You were right. He didn't accept. Said he was busy. What can he be doing when he's broke?"

"Maybe he was writing application letters," Sam said, to save her friend's feelings. Busy with a dog, she added to herself. She was slightly cheered that at least he wasn't going out with other women.

Jake didn't call the next day either. Sam found she had plenty of free time, with Rue on holidays. One afternoon, she decided to visit Alberry Drive to see how Beckie was getting along. She wouldn't be overly friendly to Jake, but she wouldn't be cold, either. She had no intention of letting him see she was hurting. If he wanted to be just friends, then that's what they'd be. Nothing wrong with saying hello to a friend and seeing how he was making out with the dog she had promised to keep an eye on.

As soon as Sam rang the bell, she heard Beckie's yelps and heard her scratching at the door. Jake wasn't far behind the dog.

"Sam!" he exclaimed. His first rush of pleasure lent an eager note to his voice and brought a wide, lopsided smile to his face. He noticed at once that Sam wasn't smiling.

"Hi, Jake," she said with what she hoped was a natural look. "I hope I'm not disturbing you. I just dropped in to see if Beckie's all right. I told Rue I would." She picked the dog up, using her as an excuse not to look at Jake. The dog wagged her tail and squealed in delight, stopping only to lick Sam's fingers.

Jake said, "I hope you don't feel you need an excuse to call. Come on in. Have some coffee."

Sam strolled into the office. The terminal was on, with a scrawl of numbers running across it. She found the office unutterably dreary. He hadn't added a single thing since the last time she'd been here.

Jacob felt defensive when he noticed her looking around. What must Sam think of this dump? She was used to the best. Suddenly he wanted to get away from these reminders of his failure.

"I was just going to take Beckie for a walk," he said. "I could use a break myself."

"Then I guess I can forget about that coffee, huh?" she said coolly. Boy, he was really anxious to get rid of her! What did he think she was going to do? Try to sell him some furniture?

His look of surprise told her she had misunderstood. "I hoped you'd come with us," he said. "We'll stop at the donut place. I'm out of cream."

"I take my coffee black, actually." He didn't even remember. She remembered he took two creamers, no sugar. "But since I came to see Beckie, let's go for that walk. How's she behaving?"

"Just the way you said. Eating everything she can get her teeth on. I plan to train her, when I get time. I'll give her an obedience lesson tonight."

Tonight, when he'd told Ginnie he was busy. He was sitting home with the darned dog, just as she suspected. She felt a softening stab of sympathy. It was just Jake's stupid pride that was making him act this way. Maybe she could convince him she didn't expect to be showered with diamonds.

"How's the program going?" she asked.

"Oh, great. I added Mr. Wrench, as you suggested, and a Mr. Bigbucks, a stockbroker."

"I meant the program for the Regency Tower."

"Oh! I thought you were talking about our program, the Marriage Game." He looked self-conscious, as if he was sorry he'd mentioned it. Was it that thoughtless *our program* that embarrassed him? Probably just that he'd been playing with his computer, when he should have been working. "How are you doing, Sam?"

"Fine. A little slow, with Rue away. I do a lot of work for her, other stuff besides just shopping. You know, personal errands." That sounded demeaning, as if she was just a rich lady's gofer. "I'm looking after her apartment while she's gone. You know, handling her phone messages and mail," she added, although that was hardly an improvement.

"She has a high opinion of you. Says she doesn't know what she'd do without you."

"She'd find someone else, I expect. Have you got Beckie's leash?"

Jake put on the leash and they went out into the sunlight. Suddenly the neighborhood looked abysmally shabby to Jake. The streets were littered with papers and cigarette boxes and even a few beer cans. The sharp contrast to Sam's fashionable neighborhood made him almost angry.

"I plan to move out of here as soon as I can afford it," he said.

"What's your hurry? It must save money, being able to live in your office."

"If you can call it living. It must seem pretty grim to you."

"I'd fix the place up a bit, if it were mine. It wouldn't cost much. A couple of hundred."

"I guess I could swing that."

"Maybe even less. You know, secondhand stores and garage sales. Oh, speaking of garage sales, I'm having one on Saturday. Ginnie and I and another friend. It's at Ginnie's place, where we went to the party. Her mom has a whole garage full of furniture. Why don't you drop by?"

"What time?"

"We start at eight. No early birds. The good stuff'll be gone by nine."

They didn't stop for coffee immediately. Jake wanted to give Beckie a good workout, to calm her down. They walked south, toward the downtown for twenty minutes, then back via the park.

"I'll take Beckie home and put her inside," Jake said. "I wouldn't want anyone to dognap her while we're in the coffee shop. She should be quiet at home now."

"We can have our coffee at your place," she suggested.

Jake looked apologetic. "You deserve better, Sam." He smiled ruefully. "You really deserve better than the donut shop, too."

"Don't be such a snob, Jake," she said angrily, and kept walking toward his house.

"Snob?" he demanded. "I'm not a snob! What have I got to be snobbish about?"

"Pride, then. You shouldn't be ashamed of where you live. There's nothing wrong with it. And you are a snob, too! You think you're better than I am just because you're poor. Well, I work just as hard as you do. I'm not living off my father. I haven't taken a cent from him since he bought me the van. Yes, he's rich, and since I'm his only child, he wants to give me things, to make up for—"

Jake frowned and unlocked the front door. "To make up for what?" he asked.

"For never being there when I needed a father," she said gruffly, and went inside. When Sam turned her head toward the window, Jake thought maybe she was hiding her tears and knew she'd want privacy.

"I'll get the coffee," he said. Alone in the kitchen, he began to revise his opinion of Sam. Maybe he was a snob, feeling superior because he'd worked his way through college. Being born into a rich or poor family was fate, the hand life dealt you. It was up to you how you played the hand. He'd done all right for himself, barring this temporary slough.

And Sam had done all right, also. It was true she worked hard. Too darned hard to please him. If her dad wanted to ease his guilty conscience by buying her a van and setting her up in a fancy apartment—well, frankly he'd rather have had his own poor dad, who was at least there, encouraging and praising him when he needed it.

How would he have turned out if no one had cared whether he made good or not? Despite his experience, he hadn't handled money all that wisely when he finally got his hands on some. He'd bought that expensive car to impress a woman who was just using him. Well, he did love the car, of course. But he wished he had that money in his pocket now.

He waited until the coffee was made, then poured it into the paper cups and took it into the office. Sam sat on the floor, holding Beckie in her lap and stroking her as if she were a baby. Sam looked about ten years old and sad.

She looked up and smiled wanly. "I never had a dog," she said. "I always wanted one. It would have been good company. Dad got me a big life-size stuffed dog. I talked to it, but it wasn't the same, of course."

"Why couldn't you have one?"

"Mom said I was too young to look after one, and when she died, the housekeeper said a dog would wreck the furniture. I still can't have one. My apartment doesn't allow them."

"It's funny, Rue's does," he mentioned.

"Those are condominiums. They make their own rules. Lots of the residents have pets."

"I hope you'll come real often to visit Beckie." She looked at him as if waiting for something. "And me," he added. Then she smiled softly. The warmth of her smile touched a chord in him. "That's an apology, Sam. I was out of line the other night," he added softly.

"Yes, you were," she agreed, but with no ill humor. "We all make mistakes." She took the coffee he held out to her. "So, are you coming to our garage sale?"

"Is anyone selling a bed? That floor's getting pretty hard."

"I'm almost sure Ginnie's mom has one in the garage. She'd let you have it for nothing. Her husband is always grousing that there isn't room for the family cars in the garage."

"Nope, I'm not accepting charity, but I have nothing against a bargain."

"Then I'll give you a good price on a nearly new comforter I'm selling. And some coffee mugs," she added, frowning at the paper cup.

Jake nodded. "I've been feeling guilty about adding to the pollution. I made sure they were biodegradable at least. Not foam."

Sam looked around the room, thinking of how it could be improved for Jake's comfort. "You could put a throw over the bed and make it look like a sofa. You know, with lots of cushions piled up behind it along the wall. Ginnie has a little side table, and I have some really cute lamps you could use for reading. Nancy has a kilim rug." She looked up and smiled apologetically. "And Jake doesn't have any money. Sorry for dangling that temptation in front of you."

"I'll be there, anyway. I still have a few shekels. And of course the coffee lures me."

His glowing eyes suggested Sam was the main attraction. She was glad she'd come. Maybe she and Jake would never be more than friends, but a real friend was valuable.

"I'll be on the lookout for you," Sam said.

She set Beckie aside, finished her coffee and stood up. "Now I have to get back to check my messages. I do work, occasionally."

"The condo management company has its monthly meeting tonight. By tomorrow I'll know whether they're taking my program. If they do, I'll take you out for a dinner. Deal?"

"Deal. And it doesn't have to be at the Napoli Garden."

"What's that?"

"Just the ritziest restaurant in town. Personally, I'd be just as happy with pizza or Kentucky Fried Chicken."

Jake accompanied her to the door, holding on to Beckie by the collar, since she seemed to think it was time for another walk.

"Thanks for coming, Sam." It wasn't exactly a compliment, but his warm smile seemed to make it one.

"I told Rue I would. I'll be back to check up on you."

"You do that—real soon. 'Bye now." He leaned forward and placed a light kiss on her cheek.

Sam's heart felt light as a helium-filled balloon when she left. She was glad she'd brought the problem out into the open. That was the best way. Jake had been pretty reasonable about it. He didn't try to justify his behavior. Well, how could he? He was wrong.

She was sorry he hadn't asked her out that night, until she remembered she was going out with Rob Staynor. Her car phone rang while she was on her way home. It was her senior citizens, asking her to pick up a "twin bed" video for them. They loved the old movies from the thirties, with no sex or violence. Mrs. Granger told her the Hays office wouldn't even allow a married couple to be seen in bed together in the old days. They always used twin beds.

While she was at the video store, she spotted a copy of an old Sherlock Holmes movie and took it for herself. Rob used to love Sherlock Holmes. Maybe they'd go back to her place later and watch it.

Chapter Six

Dinner at the Napoli Garden was a rare treat for Sam. She honored the occasion by wearing the new white suit she'd bought for spring. It was a blazer suit with deeply notched lapels and a short, pleated skirt. To lessen its severity, she added a jumble of colored necklaces and dangling earrings. Since Rob was tall, she could wear her high-heeled sandals.

When Rob arrived, only half an hour late, he was suitably impressed. "*Trés chic,* Ms. Sherman," he said, with an appraising look.

"I didn't know they spoke French in Chicago," she replied. "You look very elegant, too, Rob."

"Your apartment's nice. Not what I expected, somehow."

"Thanks. You used to pick me up at my grandma's house. I don't crochet afghans or hook rugs. I wish I knew how. Shall we go?"

There was a sleek, fire-engine red convertible sports car waiting in front of the building. "Wow! Is that yours?" she exclaimed. "You must be doing well in Chicago."

"The rich folks still have money to invest," he explained. "That never changes."

"In that case, I'll feel free to order something expensive."

"To make up for all the hamburgers I fed you in high school." He held the door and she slid onto the leather seat.

Even the parking attendant at the restaurant was impressed with the car. His eyes widened in pleasure at the thought of parking it. "Treat her gently," Rob said to him. "I don't want her dinted before she's even paid for."

The maître d' who welcomed them was wearing a black formal suit that set the tone for the Napoli Garden. The tables were covered in red linen; vases of freshly cut flowers and hurricane lamps added to the romantic aura. In the background, the plangent strum of a soft guitar blended with the hum of conversation and the discreet clink of cutlery on china. At a quarter to nine, most of the tables were filled. They were shown to one of the choice locations that had a view of a recreation of a Roman fountain, complete with stone fish, spewing a rippling waterfall from its mouth.

"It would be a sacrilege not to start with an Italian wine and some antipasto," Rob said, studying the menu.

He ordered the escargots, Sam chose the vegetables and anchovy dip. Conversation was easy. They reminisced and caught up on what their old schoolmates were doing.

"Remember the time we sent the greased pig on to the field when we were playing football against Buffalo?" Rob asked, sending them both off into peels of laughter. "Talk about trying to catch a pigskin!"

"And the time you had to give a speech in the auditorium for Memorial Day," Sam reminded him.

"Gadies and lentlemen," Rob said, and groaned. "I practiced that speech for days, then stood up in front of five hundred people and and made a fool of myself with that spoonerism."

It was a pleasant meal. Sam laughed a lot, until she noticed that a man in the shadows around the edge of the room kept turning to look at her.

"Maybe we're upsetting the customers," she said.

"Yup, you can dress us up, but you can't take us out," Rob said, and laughed again.

Again the man turned and stared at them. Sam took another look and nearly fell off her chair. It was Jake Foster! In the Napoli Garden, the most expensive restaurant in Findley Falls! And he wasn't alone. His slender wallet even allowed him to take a date with him. Jake nodded his head; Sam gave a shocked little smile and waved. From that point on, she didn't really appreciate the food or wine. She was too busy trying to get a look at Jake's date.

Over her fettuccine she decided the woman was a blonde. Her low-cut dress and Jake's glistening white shirtfront told her it was no casual date. In fact, it was a special occasion. That bucket of ice by their table held champagne. He pretended he could hardly afford a cup of coffee, and here he was out drinking champagne with a blond beauty at a fancy restaurant. At least Sam assumed the woman was a beauty, to have made Jake lose his head to this extent.

She was furious with him for having misled her. On top of everything else, he had refused to go out with Ginnie because he was busy. Now Sam knew just what he was busy at. And what had he done with Beckie? She watched Jake and his date surreptitiously, while trying to keep up a sensible conversation with Rob. Fortunately the evening had reached the stage when Rob wanted to boast a little about his own success. All she had to do was say "Isn't that wonderful!" and "That's great, Rob," at the proper intervals.

From the corner of her eye, she noticed that Jake and his date didn't seem to be having a particularly enjoyable time. There was none of the laughing and talking that was going on at her table. No hand holding, no intimate glances, either. In fact, the blond beauty seemed a little miffed. She was leaning toward Jake, talking persuasively. Jake shook his head and said something that made her snap an angry reply. Sam was reassured, until Jake began appeasing his date. He was explaining something to her in an earnest way, leaning close, gazing into her eyes.

Sam was so intrigued she forgot to order dessert, and she had really been looking forward to the zabaglione. She just ordered a cappuccino.

"Watching your waist, are you?" Rob teased.

"If I don't, nobody else will."

"I don't think you have to worry for a few pounds yet, Sam."

"Actually I was watching the man at that table over there," she admitted, nodding to Jake.

"The one with the gorgeous blonde? I've noticed him looking at you a couple of times. Do you know him?"

"He's a friend—a customer I bought some office stuff for. A new man in town."

"I'll invite them to join us for coffee," Rob said. He was up on his feet before she had time to stop him.

"No!" she whispered loudly, but it was too late. Rob was already at the table, bowing and introducing himself. Of course it was the blonde he was really interested in. Rob was always eager to meet any new woman.

Sam watched in exquisite embarrassment as Jake spoke to his date, then reluctantly rose to follow Rob to his table, with the woman in tow.

"Sam, I'd like you to meet Angela Thurston, a business associate," Jake said. "We worked together in New York. Angela, this is Sam Sherman."

"Very happy to meet you," Angela said, taking Sam's hand. She had a man's handshake that nearly crushed Sam's fingers. Angela was pretty, but not drop-dead gorgeous, as Sam had feared. Her dress looked as if it might have a designer label, and the lightening job on her hair would cost a fortune at Antonio's salon. Sam couldn't even estimate what it would cost in New York.

"I take it Rob has introduced himself," Sam said.

The next thing that popped into her head was that Angela was the woman who had used Jake so badly at his office. She was missing him and had come back to try to get him in her clutches again.

When everyone was introduced and they were all having their coffee, they began to sort out a few details about their backgrounds.

"I'm from Findley Falls," Rob said. "I'm home on holidays. Sam and I used to be high school sweethearts." He gave her fingers a squeeze and smiled.

Angela made some suitable remark. Jake arranged his lips into a smile while glaring with his eyes, giving him the air of a martyr resigned to torture.

"What sort of work do you folks do?" Rob asked. Since he seldom took his eyes off Angela, it was she who answered.

"Computer software," she said.

"Angela's found herself a very interesting job in Chicago," Jake added.

"I'm trying to talk Jacob into joining me," she said. "We always worked so well together."

Sam gave a sharp look to Jake, who refused to acknowledge it. He was adding sugar to his coffee and stirring it with unnecessary concentration. Jake didn't take sugar in his coffee. He usually took only cream.

"Chicago!" Rob exclaimed. "That's where I'm working."

"What do you do, Rob?" Angela asked, with a certain eagerness that hinted she wasn't reluctant to enlarge on the acquaintance.

"I'm a stockbroker."

From that point on, it was mainly Rob and Angela who did the talking.

"Oh, a stockbroker!" Angela said, with warm approval. "Who do you work for?"

It was patently obvious that Jake was unhappy with their conversation. *Jealous* didn't seem too strong a word. And if he was jealous, then he'd probably go running off to Chicago with Angela, to keep her from Rob. Since the other couple was deeply engrossed in discussing Chicago, Sam decided she could have some private conversation with Jake. She didn't intend to show the least interest in whether or not he went to Chicago, however. And she certainly didn't intend to remind him he was supposed to be watching his pennies.

"How's Beckie?" she asked.

"She chewed my favorite jersey to pieces and wet the kitchen floor."

"Time for those obedience lessons."

"She's unteachable." His eyes turned to Rob. He was exactly the kind of man he thought Sam would like. Successful, handsome, outgoing. "So you and Rob are old sweethearts," he said.

"From high school, years ago."

"He seems like a nice guy," Jake said, bracing himself to admit it.

"Oh yes, everybody likes Rob." Including Angela, she noticed.

"How long is he staying in town?"

"A week. He's going to England for his second week's holidays."

"Are you going with him?"

Her mouth fell open in shock. "What kind of a question is that?" she asked angrily.

"A simple, straightforward question. A yes or no answer will do."

Her eyes sparked angrily. "How about a none of your business answer?"

Instead of apologizing, as Sam expected, Jake went into a tirade. "Rue's counting on you to look after her place. And you promised her you'd keep an eye on Beckie. I hope you don't plan to walk away from your obligations."

"I don't need lessons in fulfilling my obligations from you."

"If you were counting on me to fill in for you, I should mention Angela's offered me a very good job in Chicago."

"And will you take Beckie with you?" she retaliated.

"No, I'd have to make some other arrangements, obviously."

From the corner of her eye, Sam noticed that Rob and Angela were exchanging business cards and even scribbling their home phone numbers on the back.

She gave Jake a derisive smile. "You'd better get your friend away from Rob."

"Afraid of the competition, Sam?" he taunted.

"No, but I thought you might be, since you've already been taken by Angela once."

He frowned. "What are you talk—Angela's not the woman I told you about."

"Oh, I see." He hadn't told her about this one.

Jake soon mentioned he had work to do and led Angela away.

"Nice woman," Rob said. "We're going to get together in Chicago. She didn't know the city and took an apartment in a kind of rough neighborhood. Your friend Jake—he isn't engaged to her or anything, is he?"

"Not to my knowledge, but I don't really know him all that well. Shall we go?"

Rob called for the bill and they left. Jake and Angela were just leaving when Rob's car arrived. Sam noticed Jake looking at the red roadster. Angela was looking, too, with interest. She waved as Rob drove away with a rather violent spinning of tires.

Sam really didn't feel like watching the Sherlock Holmes movie. She wanted to be alone to sort out her thoughts. As she had already mentioned it to Rob, however, and he was looking forward to it, she could hardly reneg. He came up to her apartment.

"You don't mind if I change into something comfortable, Rob? I don't want to get my white suit too wrinkled."

"Go ahead. I'll kick off my shoes and take off my jacket. Have you got any popcorn?"

"Only unpopped. I can make some, if you like."

"What good's a movie without popcorn?"

Sam changed into a comfortable jersey and shorts, since the weather was becoming warm. It was fun, making the popcorn with Rob. The movie was also enjoyable. Rob really was just a friend. She realized when she was with him how much more than a friend Jake had become. There was no sexual tension with Rob, just easy conversation and laughs. It was fun, but there was no undercurrent of excitement. Rob could praise Angela to the skies, and she didn't give a hoot.

As soon as the movie was over, Rob rose and stretched. "I think *A Scandal in Bohemia* is my favorite Holmes tale," he said. "It's 'The Woman' that does it. That's the only story where Sherlock shows any interest in a woman."

"There's something to be said for romance," she agreed.

Rob was just picking up his coat when Sam's buzzer sounded. "Who can that be, at this hour of the night?" she asked. She could only think of one person—Jake. She pressed the button to let him into the building. But what if it wasn't him? "Would you mind sticking around in case it's an undesirable?" she asked Rob.

"Sure, but you can take a peek through the peephole before you let anyone in."

She ran to the door when the second buzzer sounded. It was Jake, as she thought. She opened the door and let him in. He had taken off his jacket, but still wore his dress shirt and tie.

"Sam, I'd like to talk to you, if—" He looked into the living room and saw Rob, in his shirtsleeves and stocking feet. "I'm sorry if I'm interrupting anything," he said, but his rising color said he was more angry than sorry. "I should have phoned first. I didn't realize you still had company, Sam."

She sensed a hint of accusation in that word *still*. What right did he have to censure her behavior?

Before she could respond, Rob said, "I'm just leaving." He looked questioningly at Sam. When she nodded, he put on his jacket and shoes.

"It was a lovely evening, Sam," he said. "I'll call you before I leave town." He gave her a peck on the cheek, said good-night to Jake and left.

"What did you want, Jake?" Sam asked. Her cool tone said "This better be good."

"I wanted to explain about tonight."

She shrugged. "What's to explain?"

He ran his fingers through his hair, adding to its disarray. "About my being at that expensive restaurant when I've been—"

She cut him off short. "You don't have to explain anything to me. I was there, too, remember?"

"Yes, but you haven't been complaining about being broke."

"Yes, I have. What you mean is that in my case, my escort was paying."

"So was mine," he said. "That's really what I wanted to tell you. It wasn't a date—it was business.

Angela's company sent her up here to try to woo me to going to Chicago."

"Jake! That's wonderful!" she exclaimed. Her first thought was that his financial worries were over. "Is it a good job?" She noticed that Jake didn't look as happy as he should.

"The pay's good," he said.

"You're worried about that house you rent? You can probably sublet it. Houses to rent are in short supply in town."

"Yes, I could do that," he said doubtfully. Something in his eyes told her there was another reason why he hesitated to leave. The way he was looking at her suggested that she might be the reason.

She invited him into the living room. It was beginning to look as if she and Jake had some serious talking to do. The empty popcorn bowl sat on the table. Two beer cans were beside it. Her shoes were on the floor. The scene suggested a certain intimacy. She noticed Jake's scowl as he looked around. It was her apartment, however, and she certainly didn't have to apologize to Jake for entertaining a friend.

They sat down on the leather love seat. It was the same room where she and Rob had been perfectly comfortable, but Sam wasn't comfortable now. She was on pins and needles, wondering if Jake would take the job.

"I see I interrupted your, uh, visit with Rob," Jake said in a stiff voice.

"That's all right. He was just leaving, anyway."

"Does he come home often?"

"Three or four times a year. Why?"

"Just curious. He seems very successful. A stockbroker, fancy car. Trips to Europe."

"Yes, he's doing very well for himself."

"You didn't tell me whether you plan to go to England with him." His tone made it a question. He tried to keep it light, but his swift, shallow breaths betrayed him. He stared at her with such intense concentration that she could almost feel the tension in the air.

If he was genuinely interested in her relationship with Rob, Sam decided he deserved an answer. "I'm not going to England. Rob's an old friend, Jake. That's all. We were watching a video."

"Oh." The tension eased. Jake relaxed into a more natural expression. "Not that it's any of my business." But his expression said he did make it his business. Sam felt a curl of excitement in her breast.

"What about this job?" she asked. "Is there some special reason you're not eager to take it?"

"The thing is, I really wanted to start my own company. Working for someone else is safe—a paycheck every week, security. But in this market, it's not as safe as it used to be. I never thought my old company would go bankrupt. I'm kind of excited about working on my own. That way I can control the expenditures.

"In New York, they had unnecessarily lavish offices, big expense accounts. They could have held on if they'd been more thrifty. I thought if I got the Regency Tower job, I might sell that program to some company. They give you an advance and royalties, like selling a book. You never get rich working for someone else. You have to take the risk—go on your own. Money would be tight for a while. What do you think, Sam?"

Sam's heart slowed to a thud. Here she had thought she was the reason he was hesitating to accept the job, that he didn't want to leave her. But all he was thinking about was his career, making a lot of money.

"I'm hardly the one to advise you. I don't know much about software. Why don't you talk it over with Angela?"

"I tried to, but she's biased. She painted a doom and gloom picture. I think business will bounce back. Everyone knows computers are the future. She just wants me to work for her company. She liked the Marriage Game, by the way. She's going to try to sell it to her boss as a novelty item."

Our game had become the Marriage Game. "Is that what the company she works for does, video games?"

"It's a big outfit. They're into all sorts of different areas, including business programs. They might even be interested in my condo program."

"How long can you hang on, financially?"

Jake raked his hand through his hair in a gesture she was coming to recognize. "If I sell my car, I can stick it out for half a year without selling a program. Maybe even replace my car with an old, used one. Would you be ashamed to be seen with me?"

"I told you, I'm not a snob."

He looked around the room. "No, you're not, but you're used to nice things and nice places—like the Napoli Garden."

"I've only been there twice."

She offered Jake a drink, but he refused.

"It's late. I shouldn't have come over at this hour of the night. I'll go home and sleep on this problem."

"When do you have to give Angela your answer?"

"They want somebody right away. That's the hard part. If I could hold them off for a few months, I'd do it, but they need somebody immediately. She's leaving tomorrow. I have to let her know by noon."

"You'll let me know what you decide?"

Jake gave her a strange look. "Of course. Why do you think I came to talk it over with you?"

"I'm afraid I wasn't much help."

"The trip was still worthwhile," he said, with an uncertain smile. "Maybe I was just a little curious to find out how things stood between you and Rob."

Sam's heart began to beat faster at this promising start. "Now you know," she said encouragingly.

"Yes, now I know." He sounded contented, even happy, but he didn't go on to take advantage of her availability. "It's late. I'd better let you get to bed."

He placed a quick kiss on her cheek and left. After he had gone, Sam thought about his visit as she tidied up the apartment. The only personal thing he'd said was that he was curious about her and Rob. That could indicate that he wanted to know if she was available, except that he made no move to claim her for himself. It was all pretty tentative. For all she knew, he might phone her tomorrow and say, "I've decided to take the job in Chicago after all, Sam. A bird in the hand— It's been nice knowing you."

If that's all it was, why had he come over here so late, making jealous noises? Acting as if he were not just a casual friend, but her boyfriend. He was a complicated man this Jake Foster.

Chapter Seven

Sam heard the bad news before Jake. She went to Rue's apartment the next morning at eleven to check her mail and phone messages, as agreed. The wedding invitation from Marj Spencer had arrived, so she phoned Rue in Paris to tell her the date.

"Not till the end of June? That's good, then I won't have to rush home. I'm having a marvelous time. Will you fill in the RSVP and mail it for me? And you can start to look around for a wedding present. Something silver or crystal—you know the sort of thing."

"Okay. Will do. So what are you up to in Paree?"

"I'm having a ball. Wait till you see the suit I bought for autumn. And the food! My masseuse will be furious with me. Anything interesting on my answering machine?"

Sam gave her the messages. "Will you handle them for me, darling? Let Ruth Waring know I won't be available for the weekend in New York. Her number's in my personal phone book, the little black one there by the phone."

"Yes, it's right here. I'll phone her."

"Good. Oh, and I forgot to cancel my appointment with my dentist, Dr. Lattimer. It's for next week—only a cleaning, so it can be put off. Get me an appointment in late June. Not the weekend of the wedding."

"I'll take care of it."

"You're a lifesaver. How's Beckie making out with that nice Jacob Foster?"

"She's fine, Rue. I'm keeping an eye on her."

"I'm terribly sorry the condo didn't take his computer program. Annie phoned me last night after the meeting. It's the increase in our tax bill that's the culprit."

Rue continued for a few minutes, explaining that they liked the idea of having a computer, but at this time it was just a little more than they could afford.

Sam didn't hear much after the first disastrous announcement. They weren't buying Jake's program. He was depending on that sale. He might even turn down the Chicago job on the strength of it. She hated to be the bearer of bad news, but she decided to drive out to Alberry Drive right away and tell him.

She didn't even wait to phone Ruth Waring or to set up a new appointment with the dentist. She'd come back and do that after. Sam's mood was glum as she made the drive to the northern suburb. As if to match her mood, the sky was a dull gray blanket, threatening rain any moment. Gusts of wind sent dust and dry leaves scurrying in circles to herald a storm. A few fat drops landed with a plop on her windshield just as she pulled into Jake's driveway. At least Jake was home. His car was in the driveway.

She figured Beckie must have alerted him to her arrival, because he was at the door to meet her. The rain was coming faster now. She put a spare jacket she kept in the van over her head and darted to the doorway. Beckie's welcome was boisterous, as usual. Jake's was more subdued.

His smile seemed forced as he showed her in. Jake looked as if he hadn't slept much. There were purple smudges under his eyes. His mussed hair looked as if he had been running his fingers through it.

"Come on in, Sam. I can sure use some cheering up on a miserable day like this."

She figured he was referring to the weather. "I'm afraid what I have to say won't cheer you much," she said, trying to break the bad news gently.

Jake's body stiffened, as if he were bracing himself to be hit in the stomach. He even turned pale. "More bad news?" he asked in a choked voice, and made a sound between a laugh and a croak. It was Rob, the stockbroker. He knew it! She was going to England with him after all. "This is my lucky day. Come on in."

She followed him into the office. He had arranged his former desk of a table on two pieces of tree trunk to provide a makeshift sofa, with a sleeping bag to pad it. He noticed Sam looking at the dreary setup. God, no wonder she didn't want to continue seeing him. The place was a mess. Pride forced him to make light of it.

"How do you like my redecorating?" he asked.

"Very ingenious, Jake." She tried the "sofa" and gave a weak smile.

He wheeled the chair over for her. "Nothing but the best for my guests," he said. Sam moved to the chair and he took her place on the sofa bracing himself to hear the bad news.

"So, what's brought you out in this weather?" he asked, trying for a hearty tone.

Sam looked at him with her big green eyes, cleared her throat and said, "I stopped at Rue's apartment this morning. I phoned her in Paris."

Jake frowned. Rue? What did she have to do with Rob Staynor? It was England Rob was going to, not France.

"The condo management met last night," she said.

"Oh, so you've heard. I got the word unofficially myself. Mrs. Lavin hasn't been in touch yet, but I had a call from Ned, the janitor, an hour ago."

"So you know!" Sam was surprised he was taking it so well. It was incredible, but he almost seemed relieved. Maybe he'd been dreading to tell her.

"Yeah. I heard right after I called Angela and turned down the job in Chicago. Never rains but it pours."

"Oh Jake! I'm sorry. I hoped I'd get here before you did something rash."

He reached out and took her two hands in his, while Beckie frisked about the floor, trying to discover a way to get onto the sofa. "That was thoughtful of you, Sam. I appreciate it."

"I'm just sorry I'm too late."

"You're not too late to provide a shoulder to cry on."

But Jake didn't seem in any danger of crying. If she didn't know how important that condo deal was to him, she'd almost think he was happy. "Maybe you could phone Angela again, tell her you've changed your mind," she suggested.

"I've been thinking about what I should do." He released her hands and raked his fingers through his hair. "One swallow doesn't make a summer, Sam. And one fallen leaf doesn't make an autumn. The program's good. They liked it. In fact, they plan to take it later in the year. It was the increase in taxes that caught them short. If I sell my car, I can hang on. I've definitely decided to stay in Findley Falls." A smile crinkled the corners of his eyes. "The people are so nice," he said, gazing intently at her until she felt a warm flush brighten her cheeks.

"There are lots of other big apartment buildings in town," she said. "Maybe some of them would be interested."

"I plan to visit every one of them. I'd better do that before I sell my wheels. I'll need my car, since it'll involve a lot of driving."

"I can drive you."

"You have your own business to look after. I don't want to bankrupt you, as well as myself. One of us has to be able to buy coffee."

"You know where you can stop for a coffee—anytime, Jake."

"Next time I'll phone. I wouldn't want to barge in on another date. I felt like an idiot."

"We were just watching a video."

"But you were wearing those cute shorts."

"You don't watch TV in your new suit!"

"And you were having a beer and popcorn. My lurid imagination turned it into an orgy. I really want to apologize. At least you didn't serve him *our* drink—coffee." He laughed at the absurdity of it, but his voice was low, soft, as if sharing coffee were an intimate thing. "Speaking of coffee, would you like some?"

"Sure." She remembered Jake putting sugar in his coffee last night. He'd been pretty upset to see her out with Rob. Yet he was certainly in no hurry to ask her not to see other men.

She went into the kitchen with him, accompanied by Beckie. Jake had picked a little bouquet of forsythia. The flowers sat on the window ledge in a paper cup, trying bravely to bring a touch of beauty to the dingy room. For some reason, Sam felt a big lump rise in her throat. He saw where she was looking and gave a sheepish smile.

"I stole them from the park," he admitted. "They reminded me of Mom. She had those yellow flowers growing all along the back fence at home. She'd always bring some into the house when they bloomed, since she spent most of her time inside." Jake wore a sad, nostalgic expression as he told her about it. "One of my jobs was to keep them trimmed. These yellow flowers and lilacs always remind me of my mom."

"They're called forsythia," she said, blinking away the foolish tears.

"When I have a place of my own, I want a big garden, flowers and vegetables."

"Me, too. And a swing in the backyard, the old-fashioned kind that hangs on ropes from a tree, not one of those metal sets."

"You're a purist," he said approvingly. That surprised him.

"Am I? Gee, I just thought I was greedy, wanting all the things I didn't have when I was a kid."

"That's funny, isn't it, Sam?" he said musingly. "I want all the things I did have."

Sam didn't say anything for a moment, but as Jake and she exchanged a long look, it occurred to her that the differences in their backgrounds seemed to bring them closer together somehow.

"Do you think maybe money isn't everything after all?" Jake said.

"I never thought it was."

She pondered this scrap of conversation as they took their coffee back into the office. Money never had been everything to her. Jake was the one who was always harping on it. Yet his impoverished childhood had obviously been happy, or why did he want to recreate it for his own children? And her luxurious youth had been unsatisfactory, or why did she want something different?

When they sat down, Sam ignored the chair and sat on the door-sofa with Jake. He looked around for something to use as a table. "If there's a coffee table at that garage sale, I want first dibs on it," he said. "This is ridiculous."

"Could we use one of those cardboard boxes in the corner?" she suggested. When Jake pushed the box forward, she noticed he had changed watches. The thin gold one he usually wore had been replaced by a bigger, cheaper-looking chrome one with a black leather band. "What's that watch you're wearing?" she asked.

He held out his wrist. "The battery of my watch packed it in this morning. I dug this old one out, until I can get a battery. It's an old Mickey Mouse watch."

"Is it an original?" she asked, staring at it. It was different from the new models with a quartz movement. Bulkier, with a bigger picture of Mickey in the center.

"Yeah, my dad gave it to me. It was his when he was young. It was such a treasure he hardly ever wore it. Kept it in its box for Sundays and visits."

She took his wrist and examined the watch. "It's practically in mint condition."

"I even have the box."

"They're worth a lot of money now, Jake," she said excitedly. "You could sell it."

"Sell Mickey?" he exclaimed in horror. He looked at the watch with a fond smile. "No way. This is part of my heritage. Some kids get the family gold pocket watch when their father dies. I got Mickey Mouse." He looked up questioningly. "How much is it worth?"

"I don't know, but an original clockwork one in good condition is probably worth hundreds, maybe a thousand. I'm not sure."

Jake frowned and shook his head. "No way. You can't buy memories, and you shouldn't sell them."

"I agree," Sam said, and she meant it. "What other goodies do you have hidden away in those boxes? And here I thought you were poor."

"My baseball cards, hockey cards. A guy offered me two *K* for that collection." He looked up, grinning. "They're not for sale, either."

"You wouldn't happen to have an original Rembrandt or van Gogh with no sentimental associations in your chest of souvenirs?"

"Nope, not even a Lou Natique. But I have a collection of original G.I. Joe dolls, and an original Batmobile and Green Hornet car—toy car, of course. They're not in very good condition, but the nicks and scratches only make them more valuable to me. My sister still has her collection of Barbie dolls. We're a family of pack rats."

Sam listened in a daze. Where had she gotten the idea Jake was only interested in money? He was more sentimental than she was. She hadn't saved her old toys. She had piled them all into boxes—dozens of expensive dolls and toys of all sorts—and had taken them to the charity thrift shop when she'd left home, and had felt almost a sense of relief to be rid of them.

"If something has to go," he said, "and it obviously does, then it'll be the new car. I'm coming to dislike it quite thoroughly, anyway. It reminds me of my spendthrift ways. Off it goes to the used car dealer. Let some other poor sap waste his money on it."

"You'd probably make more on a private sale."

"That's true. It'd take a little longer to sell, but it'd be worth it. Of course I may starve in the meantime, but thin people live longer." He was joking, of course, but Sam wondered if he was actually going hungry. She knew he'd never admit it if he was.

"I don't want to step on your machismo, Jake, but if you're really short, I could lend you a couple of hundred. I figure I'll make that much on the garage sale."

"I'm not offended. I'm flattered, but if the situation becomes desperate, I could always sell my good watch for a couple of hundred. At the moment a decent bed is becoming more important than a gold watch."

"If it's just a status symbol you're after, wear your original Mickey Mouse," she said. "But take good care of it. Is there any chance Angela's company might take the Marriage Game?"

"Oh, didn't I tell you? They hated it. Thought it was sexist. Degrading to women, to suggest they chased men. And if I changed it to make men chasing women, as I suggested, that'd be turning women into objects. It's a lose-lose situation. They've been getting flak for the violence of some of their games, so they're sensitive to issues, Angela says." He laughed as if it were a good joke, but beneath the laughter, Sam thought she detected a note of panic.

"We're living in a politically correct world. Would it be overly sensitive to make the game one of chasing the buck?" Sam asked. "The Great American Dream. You know, two men racing each other, trying to make a million, meeting obstacles. Losing their jobs, their stocks crash, or the stocks split and increase in value."

Beckie finally managed to reach the sofa. She emitted a long sigh and placed her head on Jake's lap. He ran his fingers through her long hair, enjoying its roughness against his fingers. Watching him, Sam felt a little jealous of Beckie.

"The games are just a hobby," he said. "I'll concentrate on trying to sell the condo program for the time being. You know what they say, it's always darkest before the dawn." He gave his lopsided grin. "I know all the clichés."

"When the going gets tough, the tough get going."

"If at first you don't succeed, try again. I think we both get the idea."

The atmosphere was so congenial, despite the bad news, that Sam hated to leave. She felt a new closeness to Jake. He was showing her a vulnerable side of himself she hadn't seen before. The way he spoke of his parents and his childhood had revealed unsuspected depths of sensitivity. She didn't think he showed that side to many people, just to special friends. She also admired the toughness beneath the vulnerability. He wasn't ready to throw in the towel at the first blow. He'd stick it out and be a success one day. And he'd do it on his own terms, not by rushing off to the first job offered. As the storm petered out, however, she figured she'd better get back to work.

Jake walked her to the door, with Beckie yelping frantically in hopes of a walk. "Are you free tonight?" Jake asked.

"I'm taking the stuff for the garage sale over to Ginnie's. You're welcome to come."

She thought his hesitation was probably due to Ginnie's having asked him out. It might be a little embarrassing for them both. "Or I could give you a call when I get home. It won't be late. Maybe you could come over to my place. I'll get a video."

"A tempting offer, but I'd better keep my nose to the grindstone. I have a lot of work to do."

"I'll let you get at it, then," she said. "See you at the garage sale." On an impulse, she reached up and kissed him lightly. "Don't worry, Jake. Things'll turn out all right."

"They better. I've just burned my bridge behind me."

"Who wants to retreat, anyway?" she asked.

"Not tough guys like us." He brushed his fingers lightly over her cheek, leaving a trail of tingles behind. "You're very soft, for a tough guy, Sam," he said tenderly. His fingers traced the edges of her lips until they quivered. Then he lowered his head and kissed her, just a fleeting kiss, like the flutter of a moth's wing. He had to tense his body to stop from doing more.

She saw his Mickey Mouse watch from the corner of her eye and thought that Jake also had his soft side.

He opened the door. She had to slip out quickly to prevent Beckie from following her.

Jake went to the window to watch her leave. His gloom had left him, to be replaced by a feeling of euphoria. She wasn't going to England with Rob. That was the main thing. He would really have felt like a fool if he had turned down the Chicago job to be near Sam and she'd left him high and dry.

So he'd lost a customer, he'd find others. He'd always been too uptight about work, too concerned with security. Money wasn't everything. He'd learned that from Sam. She was good for him.

After her van had turned the corner, he went out to examine his car. He hadn't been so cautious with his money when he'd bought this beauty. And look where it had got him. Flat busted when he lost his job. He wasn't in the same position as Sam, not by a long shot. She had her rich father to fall back on. He only had himself. Had he been stupid to turn down the Chicago offer? Sam said money wasn't all that important to her, and she seemed to mean it. But dammit, he wished he could take her out to nice places.

She might not think she wanted money, but that was only because she was so used to having it that it seemed unimportant. She didn't really believe it. "The American dream," she had said about that millionaire game. And it was. If she had to scrape along on peanuts for any length of time, she'd soon become tired of it. This survival business was a game for her. For him it was deadly serious.

He wiped the raindrops from his car and went back inside to start working the phone. It didn't really make much sense to approach the apartment janitors first. They weren't the ones who made the decisions. What he had to do was find out who owned the apartment buildings and approach the managers. Now, who would know that? Everything was made more difficult by his being a stranger in town. Maybe the Chamber of Commerce could help him.

He made an appointment with a Mr. Peter Paulson at the C of C for later that same morning. That meant getting dressed in business clothes. It turned out that six of the larger buildings were owned by the Holden Corporation and managed by someone called Felix Ungar. When Jake finally got hold of his office, Mr. Ungar was out of town for the remainder of the week. His secretary made an appointment for Monday morning at ten. Jake had a hamburger and went back home.

With nothing better to do, he began fooling around with the millionaire game Sam had suggested, just for fun. It was mainly kids who played these games, and they probably weren't much interested in making a million bucks. Still, you never could tell. Executive sand boxes and the Rubik's Cube had enjoyed a brief fling, to ease the tensions of the boardroom. Maybe an executive computer game would catch on long enough to make him a small bundle.

He'd start with two guys like himself losing their jobs. They'd be racing after the plum of the country's top job, at a million a year. Have to give the company a name and put plenty of pitfalls in the path to the top. He had soon lost himself in his work. The only sound in the room was the quiet click of the computer keyboard and an occasional sniff from Beckie, who was not at all amused at the lack of action.

Sam went back to Rue's apartment to call her dentist and Ruth Waring, and to fill in and mail the wedding invitation response. Rue had forgotten to ask her to water the plants, but she did that, too. The luxuriousness of Rue's rambling penthouse emphasized how dismally Jake was living. She wished she could help him somehow. Maybe her dad knew some businessmen who might hire him.

But no, Jake would hate that. He was too independent. There was really nothing she could do except lend emotional support, and if he sold his car, she'd make him let her drive him to his appointments. He couldn't afford to waste money on taxis. That and emotional support were about all she could offer.

He really seemed to appreciate her emotional support. He had looked like death when she'd arrived, but when he had someone to talk to about losing the contract, he seemed much more cheerful. She wondered why he'd turned down the Chicago job. Was it just because he wanted to work on his own or had her being in Findley Falls had something to do with it? Whatever his reason, she was glad he was staying in town. Maybe something would come of this friendship yet.

Chapter Eight

"I always thought a garage sale would be fun, but this is hard work," Nancy said, as she lifted a heavy box of coffee mugs and assorted dishes out of Sam's van. She toted them into Ginnie's garage and placed them carefully on the floor beside other sale items.

"You can't get tired yet," Sam gasped. The box of books she was carrying weighed a ton. "We still have to label everything."

Nancy stood up and stretched to ease the cramp in her back. "And be back here tomorrow at seven at the latest, to arrange the tables on the driveway."

"Think of all the money we'll make," Sam said encouragingly.

"We don't have to label everything individually," Ginnie pointed out. "We'll put similar items in boxes and just put a sign on the box, with the price for books or coffee mugs or whatever."

"And we'll have a one-dollar table, with small items on it," Sam added. "We'll each keep track of our own sales, agreed? That way we won't have to try to sort out who gets how much later on."

"What about the clothes?" Nancy asked, lifting a raincoat from a box of her used clothing. "They'd look better hanging up. Do you have anything we could use, Ginnie?"

"We'll hang the coats and dresses on the fence," Ginnie said. "On clothes hangers, I mean. The T-shirts and sweaters can go on a table, neatly folded."

"Until people start examining them," Nancy said. "I sure hope it doesn't rain."

"If it rains, we move everything into the garage," Sam said. "It won't keep the crowds away. Nothing dampens a bargain hunter's search for a bargain. Trust me. I know about bargain hunters. What do you think I should ask for this lamp?" She held up a boudoir lamp with a milk glass base and a white shade.

"Twice what you'd take," Ginnie suggested. "They'll try to bargain you down. Ask for ten, you'll get five."

"I paid twenty-five for it, just last year."

"I saw lamps going for two dollars at another sale," Nancy said.

"I'll ask for eight and take five," Sam said, writing up a label.

It was ten-thirty when they had finished their chore. They were exhausted and covered with dust. Ginnie invited them in to wash up and have a sandwich before going home. Nancy and Sam left immediately after, since they all had to be up early the next morning.

Sam set her alarm for six-thirty. She figured the extra half hour's sleep was more important than breakfast on that busy day. She could have coffee at the sale.

From seven until eight she was busy helping set up the tables. The sky was overcast, threatening rain.

"Maybe we should leave the merchandise in the garage," Nancy said, peering at the sky.

"The stuff looks better out in the daylight," Sam said. "More tempting."

Ginnie settled the matter. "We'll wait till seven-thirty. If it doesn't rain, out it goes."

"Right," Sam said. "Now, who's in charge of coffee?"

"You are," Nancy and Ginnie both replied at once.

"You didn't forget the coffee machine, Sam!" Nancy exclaimed.

"It's in the van. You get the water, Ginnie. I'll set it up."

It didn't rain, but the clouds kept the bargain hunters at bay. At seven-thirty they began to take the tables out to the driveway. At a quarter to eight, the gray sky was clearing to a dull blue when their first customer arrived. By eight o'clock, they were inundated with customers. The coffee Sam poured for herself grew cold in the cup. Between haggling with potential customers over prices and selling coffee and donuts, she couldn't find time to drink it.

One man monopolized the box of paperbacks, elbowing other customers aside. "I'll give you two bucks for the whole box," he said to Ginnie.

"There's over a hundred books in there! That's less than two cents each. The price is a quarter."

"Some of them are damaged." He lifted out one that was slighty dog-eared. Most of them were in perfect condition.

One eager customer reached in over his shoulder and pulled out a couple of recent bestsellers. She handed over her fifty cents without arguing.

Reassured that they weren't overpriced, Ginnie repeated, "The price is a quarter. Sorry." She turned to deal with a customer who was buying sweaters. The book bargain hunter shuffled off to look at other merchandise.

It was an interesting morning. Some customers haggled over one dollar items, some bought the bigger things with no haggling at all. Others just looked, asked for a few obscure items such as war memorabilia or old comic books and left when there was none of their specialty available.

Jake arrived at eight-thirty. Sam spotted him and beckoned him to her table.

"Looks like a success," he said, looking around at the eager shoppers.

"I was afraid everything would be gone by the time you got here. What are you after? Coffee mugs? A bed?"

"Both, and a few other items as well."

"The bed is Ginnie's. I'll get her. We left the big stuff in the garage."

Jake and Ginnie disappeared into the garage, where the larger items were stored. They stayed for ten minutes. When they came out, they were both smiling. Ginnie waved a fistful of bills at Sam.

Sam didn't have much time to see that Jake got what he was after. Her earrings and cast-off clothes were a great hit with the teenagers. By about ten the crowd had dwindled to a dozen stragglers, and the tables were well picked over.

"Now I can have my coffee. How about you, Jake?" Sam asked. He was browsing through a box of hardcover books Ginnie had culled from her attic.

"Great, thanks."

When she took the coffee to him, she looked to see what he was reading. It was Ginnie's high school yearbook. The picture he was looking at was the girls' basketball team, with Sam in the front row, holding the ball.

"I hardly recognized you with all that hair," he said, grinning.

"Oh, lord! I look like a sheep dog with those bangs hanging in my eyes. You would find that!"

"This is too good to pass up," he said, and tucked it under his arm to buy.

"Did you get the bed?"

"Sure did...and a coffee table and a few other items, as well."

"I saved you half a dozen coffee mugs. On the house."

"Nope, this is a fund-raising event for you needy women. I'll pay the going price."

"That'll be the grand sum of sixty cents. They're a dime each."

"Cheap at half the price. I might go whole hog and get a cream and sugar set while I'm at it. Live it right up. I saw some in that dollar box."

"You'd better move fast. The small pieces of china are selling out."

"At the prices you women are selling for, I figure a guy could furnish his house for a couple of hundred bucks. I should have come early and bought the lot."

"I didn't know you wore earrings! That was my hot seller, that and my sweaters."

He leaned down and said in a low tone, "I hocked my good watch. I'm loaded."

"I'm glad." She tilted her head to one side and added, "And sorry. That you had to sell it, I mean."

"I didn't sell it. I just pawned it. I have a month to redeem it. Keep your fingers crossed. I put an ad in the paper to sell my wheels, too. No action on that yet. The paper doesn't hit the streets until noon."

A customer came along to buy some of the hardcover books. Jake lifted the box to a now empty table for her. He found a box of records beneath it and began sorting through them. "Only a quarter?" he asked. "I'm tempted. I collect old records."

"They're a glut on the market. Everybody's using tapes or CDs nowadays."

Sam, watching him, wondered why he was examining the top cover of one album so carefully. He seemed to be trying to peel it off. Then she was distracted by a customer's questions and forgot it.

Later, Sam felt a twitch at her sleeve. Turning, she saw Jake staring with a dazed look. "Do you realize some of those records are worth big bucks?" he whispered. "I put the hardcover books back on top of them. It's a good thing they were hidden beneath those books. You've got an original Beatles *Yesterday and Today* album."

"That's great."

"It's better than great. It has the butcher cover underneath."

"Underneath what?" she asked in confusion.

"Underneath the trunk cover."

"Are you feeling all right, Jake?"

"No, I think I'm dreaming. Don't you know what this means?"

He handed her an album with the four Beatles on the cover. The record was old but in good condition. Paul was sitting in a big open trunk; the others stood behind him. Jake had carefully peeled away the corner of the jacket paper. Beneath it, there seemed to be another picture.

"This is the trunk cover," he explained, pointing to the trunk Paul was sitting in. Then, lifting the corner of the top paper carefully, he added, "and this is the butcher cover, the one that's really valuable."

"Why did they cover it?"

"Because the record company got nervous about the cover. It had raw meat on it. They figured it didn't fit the Beatles' image. This business of being issue sensitive goes back a long way. They sold a couple of hundred of the butcher covers before they took it off the market and made a new cover. It seems a few records just had the new trunk cover pasted on over the old butcher cover. These are as rare as hen's teeth. Collectors would give their right arm for this. I've never actually seen one before."

"Never mind their right arm. How much money would they give?"

"It's anybody's guess, but you can think in terms of thousands, not hundreds."

"Thousands!"

"One or two thousand, anyway," he said uncertainly.

"Oh my gosh. What luck for you, Jake. You won't have to sell your car. Snap it up quick."

He was looking through the stack. "There are other goodies here, too. An early Elvis, and some vintage

Doors. Not really valuable, but good stuff. I couldn't take any of these for a quarter each. It'd be highway robbery."

"They're Nancy's. I'll tell her. Boy, will she be glad! She's really broke."

She beckoned Nancy forward. "Jake says these records are quite valuable, Nancy," Sam said.

"Really? Maybe I should raise the price to a dollar each. What do you think, Jake?"

"Make it fifty or a hundred each," Jake said, "but don't sell this one at any price." He handed her the *Yesterday and Today* Beatles record. "It's worth real money."

Nancy blinked. "You're kidding!" She frowned. "Well, they're marked a quarter each. I guess I have to sell them for that. You got yourself a bargain, Jake."

"No, I wouldn't take them."

"That's what garage sales are all about. Finding a treasure." She looked longingly at the album. "I once got a gold bracelet for a dollar."

"Put the records away," Jake said. "If you don't want to keep them for yourself, I know a guy in New York who'd give you a thousand, maybe more, for this one record. And the others are worth something, also. Where'd you get that album, Nancy? It came out in '66. You weren't even born."

"I bought it at a used-record shop for a dollar when I was in high school. That's when I bought most of these. I only bought them because my boyfriend liked this older music. I forgot all about them when I got my tape player."

"It's a good thing you held on to them."

Nancy touched his hand shyly. "Thanks, Jake. Not many people are as honest as you. Make that generous. You had every legal right to buy it for the price marked. Most people would have snatched it up without saying a word."

When Sam smiled at Jake in that approving way, he felt he had gotten the best of the bargain.

"No, they would have tried to bargain the price down to a nickel," Sam said.

Jake picked the box up. "I'll put these in the garage," he said, taking the box away for safety.

Nancy just grinned. "You've got yourself a really nice man there, Sam. Imagine, a thousand dollars! I can stay in Findley Falls!" She hugged Sam and laughed in delight.

Sam made a sad face. "I sent all my old records off to the charity thrift shop last year. I probaby had some collectibles, too."

By eleven o'clock there was nothing of value left, and the vendors were practically giving away the rest to get rid of it. At eleven-thirty the sale was officially over.

"I'll help you put away the tables," Jake offered.

"Only if you let me buy you lunch," Nancy said. "I owe you, Jake."

"We're having lunch here," Ginnie said. "I have hamburgers and the fixings. The barbecue's all ready. Of course you'll stay, too, Jake."

"I really should be arranging to get my bed home," he said.

"No problem. It'll fit in the van," Sam said. "We may have to leave the back doors open."

Jake said, "Thanks very much, but—"

Sam knew he wanted to stay and was only hesitant to accept what he probably saw as charity. "Do stay," she said. "We need someone to cook the hamburgers while we count our money."

Jake stayed and insisted on doing the cooking. He arranged the patties on the grill, and while they cooked he set the condiments out on the table. The women did exactly what Sam had said. They counted their money. Small bills and change were arranged into piles.

"Four hundred and seventeen dollars!" Ginnie crowed. "It was Mom's furniture that did it, but she's letting me keep the money."

"I have two hundred and sixty, plus change," Sam said.

Nancy just smiled. "I have over a thousand, or will have when I sell my records. I want to celebrate, take you all out for dinner tonight."

Sam was pretty sure Jake wouldn't accept two free meals. When Nancy went over and invited him, he said, "That's very kind of you, Nancy, but I'm busy tonight."

"Sam's coming," she said to tempt him.

He just smiled. "I'll give you the name of that used-record salesman in New York. Tell him I recommended him and he'll be sure to give you a good price. I did a lot of business with him. Here, I think I have a couple of his cards in my wallet." He dug a dog-eared card out and handed it to her. "I recommend him to my friends who are interested in old records. You won't even have to send them. He tours around the state in the summer hunting out rare finds like this. Just put them away safely."

Lunch was enjoyable. The women were flushed from their success, and Jake was happy to see Sam happy. Her friends seemed like nice down-to-earth people. The beautiful house and extensive grounds told him Ginnie's family was obviously well off, but she didn't put on any airs. He always found you could judge people by the company they keep, and Sam didn't seem to go in for snobs. Occasionally his eyes strayed to the white gazebo at the end of the garden, calling up memories of his meeting there with Sam.

After lunch they loaded his furnishings into the van and Sam drove them to Alberry Drive, with Jake following in his car.

"I'll ask my next-door neighbor to give me a hand with moving the bed in," Jake said, when they reached his house. "He dropped in for a beer yesterday afternoon. He's a nice guy. He won't mind."

"It's only a single bed. You and I can carry it," Sam said. "I'm strong!"

She insisted on helping him carry in the furniture and set it up, accompanied by Beckie, who enjoyed the unusual goings-on. When they carried in the mattress, Beckie jumped up on top for a ride.

"She thinks she's Cleopatra, being hauled down the Nile," Sam joked.

"Yeah, and we're her slaves. Off you go, Cleo. We have to tilt this to get it through the door." Beckie leapt down and followed at their heels, enjoying herself immensely.

Sam enjoyed herself, too. It was fun to arrange the few bits of furniture to best advantage.

"Do you read in bed?" she asked.

"I did, when I had a lamp."

"Well, you have a lamp now, and a bedside table. We'll have to put the lamp table on the far side of the bed so the cord will reach the socket. Do you have any linen?"

"In that box," he said, pointing to a cardboad box in the corner. The sheets were stylish percales, done in a masculine pattern of black and brown stripes on a white background. They worked together to make up the bed. When it was done, they both looked at it, suddenly self-conscious.

"I'll sleep well tonight," Jake said, trying to ignore the bed's other possible use.

Sam took her cue from him. "We're all done here. Shall we go down and arrange the coffee table?"

"Yes. It'll be nice to have some place to put down our cup—or mug at least," he added. He looked a moment at the bed, then he looked at Sam. No, he wouldn't risk making a fool of himself.

They were both hot and tired after their work and opted for a beer, but the coffee table still came in handy. Beckie took a fancy to it. She curled up underneath it with her head resting on her paws and stared up at them.

"She's trying to make me feel guilty for not taking her for a walk today," Jake said. "Shall we take her, after we have our well-earned drink?"

"You take her. I have to check my calls. Saturday's a busy day for me. But it's the only day for a garage sale. I doubt I would have made two hundred and sixty dollars in commission this morning."

The phone rang while they were still drinking their beer. It was in the office that Jake used for a living room as well. He went to his desk to pick it up. "This may be a customer for my car!" he exclaimed. "That was fast! The paper's only been out a few hours.

"Angela!" he said, surprised.

Since they were in the same room, Sam could hear every word. "That's a generous offer," he said, lifting his eyebrows in pleasure. "Actually, I've pretty well decided to stay here." He looked across the room to Sam and winked. "I bought some furniture today. I'm making friends, settling in." The wink was replaced by a warm smile, directed straight at her. She knew it wasn't the bed and a couple of small tables that were keeping him in Findley Falls. It wasn't just friends, either. It was one special friend—Sam Sherman.

Sam could hear Angela's voice on the other end of the line. She sounded persuasive, and Jake was listening intently. Sam decided it wasn't right to eavesdrop and took the empty cans out to the kitchen. After a few minutes, she went to tidy up in the washroom while Jake finished his call.

When she came out, the living room was silent, so she returned. Jake had finished his call. "That was Angela, as you probably guessed," he told her. "She just came up with a very interesting offer." He didn't get specific, and of course Sam didn't ask, but his smile told her it was even more than he hoped for.

Sam suddenly felt as if her lungs were collapsing. "Are you having second thoughts?" she asked. Her voice sounded wistful.

"Nope. My mind's made up. I have an appointment with Felix Ungar on Monday."

"Who's Felix Ungar?" It immediately darted into her head that he was some other employer in another big city.

"He runs half a dozen big apartment buildings in town. I hope to sell him my program. If I get a few satisfied customers, it'll be easier to peddle it to a big company."

Her lungs expanded again. She couldn't control the smile that beamed out and didn't even bother trying. "Good. I'm glad you're staying, Jake. That was very nice of you—about the Beatles album. Nancy really wanted to treat you to dinner. You shouldn't let your pride—"

He batted the idea away. "It wasn't that. I really do have to work tonight. I have a few ideas simmering. All of a sudden, I'm very eager to get established. I think you know why." When he looked at her like that, with his heart in his eyes, Sam felt her knees turn to water.

"Don't become a workaholic," she said. She was sorry she wouldn't be seeing him that night.

"You go on out with your friends. I'll call you tomorrow morning."

Jake walked her to the door and kissed her goodbye. It was a long, warm, lingering kiss that turned her insides to melting butter and left her starry-eyed.

That afternoon she was catching up on her phone messages. Saturday was busy, as usual. None of the commissions was large or difficult, but together they kept her hopping and made her a fair profit.

She was sorry Jake wasn't along for Nancy's dinner that evening. It was enjoyable, but it would have been better with him. Nancy was so euphoric she even bought them all a margarita, with which she toasted Jake.

"Are we to understand Jake is no longer available?" Ginnie asked with a knowing grin.

Sam replied, "I plan to stake my claim, but officially he's available—if you two want to lose your best friend."

"A hard choice!" Ginnie grinned.

"Forget it," Nancy advised. "You're fighting a losing battle. Jake hardly took his eyes off Sam all morning. Didn't you notice, Ginnie?"

"I did, and vice versa," Ginnie added. "Sam watched her man like a hawk. You better let us be your bridesmaids when the time comes, Sam."

"We're not talking about marriage, for heaven's sake," Sam said. It was the first time this idea had surfaced. It took her by surprise, but she got used to it in a strange hurry. Married to Jake Foster! What would it be like?

"Hey, wake up," Ginnie said, nudging her elbow. "He hasn't asked you yet. Nancy wants to know if you want dessert. We're having a gooey, fattening, delicious hot-fudge sundae."

"Same here," Sam said, still in a daze.

When she went home that night, she realized she wouldn't say no if Jake did ask her to marry him. She could give up her apartment and use her stuff to furnish his house. Her place wasn't big enough for both of them. By the time she had mentally rearranged his office and bedroom, she shook herself back to reality.

This was crazy. She'd only known Jake for a few weeks. She knew he was honest—that was important. And hardworking. Other people liked him, too, so she wasn't just letting her hormones run away with her head. Although the hormones were certainly in sync.

Jake wasn't so crazy about money and success that he was willing to sell his sentimental souvenirs. She liked that about him, too. In fact, she couldn't think offhand of one single thing she didn't like—except that he hadn't asked her out that night. Maybe he worked just a little too hard. She could live with that.

Chapter Nine

Little bubbles of joy kept fizzing up through Sam's impatience on Sunday morning. She could hardly wait for Jake to phone so she could tell him her plan. As soon as she had looked out her window and seen the brilliant sun shining in a clear blue sky, she knew it was too fine a day to stay in the city. She had decided to have a picnic in the country with Jake.

They would go for a long drive in the countryside, stopping at some idyllic spot near a lake or stream. The park at Lake Oneida, maybe, only not at one of the public tables. She'd take a blanket, they'd eat sandwiches by a stream and drink white wine. Afterward, they'd stroll through the meadows, picking a bouquet of wildflowers: buttercups and blue-eyed grass and daisies.

Then they'd sprawl on the blanket in the shade of a willow tree. She'd pluck the petals from the daisies to find out who she was going to marry. Rich man, poor man—she didn't care which Jake was, just as long as he was her man.

Right after breakfast she dashed out to the deli and bought cold cuts, dill pickles, Swiss cheese and some imported pears. She cleaned celery and carrot sticks and put them in a plastic container, humming happily in time with the music on her radio as she prepared the lunch. She cut a long stick of crusty French bread in six pieces, then cut the pieces in two. The bread was as light as air. Layers of nut-sweet Black Forest ham shaved paper-thin were piled on, then Dijon mustard. For variety she added cheese to some of the sandwiches, pepper-seed salami to a few others. She even remembered to put the white wine in the fridge to cool down.

The fizz went out of her day around eleven, when Jake called and said he'd be busy all day. Something about a program Angela had suggested to him. He sounded excited, but Sam hardly listened.

"It's Sunday, Jake! Didn't you ever hear of a day of rest?" she asked.

"This is important, Sam. What are you doing?"

"Making sandwiches for a picnic lunch," she said, with a wistful glance at the table. "There's enough for two." Two? She'd made enough to feed a small army. "I have some fresh imported Swiss cheese and pears as well."

"Plutocrat! Are you trying to seduce me from work?" He laughed.

"A man has to eat."

"I'll send out for a pizza when I get hungry. Don't worry about me."

It obviously wasn't necessary to tell him not to worry about her. "How about Beckie? Did you remember to feed her?" she asked, trying to conceal her disappointment.

"I did, but she could do with some exercise. Are you interested in a walk?"

Sam's anger melted faster than a snowflake on a hot griddle. "I'll be right there!" she said, and hung up.

She finished the sandwiches and wrapped a few of them up, putting them and the peeled vegetables into a bag to take with her. She added a freezer pack to keep them fresh. She didn't bother with the fruit and cheese and wine. It wasn't going to be a picnic after all, but at least they'd have a quick sandwich together.

They could walk Beckie to Alberry Park and eat their lunch there. It wasn't exactly the idyllic afternoon she had had in mind. There was no babbling brook, not even a fountain, just a bunch of rowdy kids playing baseball. The few measly flower beds certainly weren't for picking; their blanket under the willows would be a hard park bench, but it was better than nothing. A lot better. She'd be with Jake. It was the company that mattered.

When she arrived, Jake came to the door, looking disheveled in an old T-shirt and faded jeans. He hadn't even bothered to comb his hair. He handed her the leash, already attached to Beckie's collar.

"Thanks, Sam. I really appreciate this," he said. "This darned dog's driving me crazy. I closed my office door, but she sits outside and whines."

Sam just stared in disbelief. "Aren't you coming with us, Jake?"

"I told you, I have to work."

She quelled the tide of anger that rose up to engulf her. How dare he make a date for her with a *dog?* "Sorry I disturbed you. Next time you can just throw out the leash, and I'll put it on Beckie myself. We wouldn't want you to waste a minute of your precious time."

He actually had the nerve to laugh! "What's the matter, Sam? Not mentioning any names, but I think somebody got up on the wrong side of the bed this morning."

"I don't have much choice. My bed's against the wall."

"That cliché isn't meant to be taken literally."

Sam had planned to share the sandwiches, but since Jake was being so impossible, she took them all to the park with her and ate alone on a park bench, feeding Beckie bits of ham. Beckie was impossible. She wanted to chase every baseball that came within a country mile of her. In the end Sam had to tether her leash to the bench, and listen to the dog yelping all through her meal. She hadn't brought anything to drink, so that every bite of the dry bread was like swallowing a golf ball. Or maybe it was the lump of anger in her throat that made her feel that way.

After lunch she went for a long walk with the dog, to work out her own frustrations. Is this how her weekends would be if she were seriously involved with Jake? Would his work always come first? Ambition was fine, but he didn't have to go overboard. He was as bad as her father—worse! At least her father sent her off to a movie or camp or for a riding lesson when he didn't have time for her.

The walk worked off her pent-up annoyance. She was just being selfish. She wasn't a child, who had to have her leisure time planned for her. And Jake wasn't her father. He was actually in desperate need of money. She knew how eager he was to get himself established.

He was probably preparing a presentation for that Felix Ungar person he'd mentioned.

She hadn't told him she'd spent the morning making a nice lunch for them. He wasn't a mind reader after all. Jake might be tired by the time she took Beckie back and be ready for a break. They'd go for a drive in the countryside, and he'd tell her all about his presentation. If he was hungry, he could eat the rest of the sandwiches. Maybe they'd stop at her apartment and get the wine as well. And the blanket...

She even managed a smile when she rang the doorbell. "We're ba-aaaaack!" she said, handing him the leash.

She felt about as welcome as the poltergeist. In fact, Jake looked at her as if he hardly recognized her. "Oh, Sam, you're back already," he said, running his hands through his hair.

Her anger flared anew. "I see you really missed us," she snipped. "We've been gone for well over an hour."

"Have you really? It only seemed like minutes. The times goes so quickly when I'm working. Can you come in for a minute?"

"Gee, I'm not sure I can spare a whole sixty seconds, Jake."

He smiled then, a real smile that crinkled the corners of his eyes and melted her anger. "I won't keep you long," he said, taking her hand and drawing her into the house. "Do you have plenty of customers today?"

"It's Sunday, Jake. I'm not working today."

"That's right," he said, frowning. "It slipped my mind."

She noticed that a day's growth of beard shadowed his jaws, adding an exciting touch of masculine roughness to his appearance. "Come on into the kitchen. I'll get us a cold drink. In fact, it must be time for lunch. Shall we order a pizza?"

"It's two-thirty. I had lunch over an hour ago."

"Is it?" He glanced vaguely at his Mickey Mouse watch and frowned. She remembered how he had had to pawn his good watch and was ambushed by a rush of pity. "So it is," he said.

Sam followed him into the kitchen. While Jake got a couple of beers from the fridge, she arranged the leftover sandwiches on a plate, wishing she'd brought the fruit. This dear man needed help.

"I made these for a picnic," she said, handing him the plate. "You haven't eaten all day, have you?"

"I think I had some cereal for breakfast." He looked at the sink. Sam didn't see any used bowl. "Maybe not," he said doubtfully.

"Are you trying to kill yourself?" she scolded, leading the way into the living room.

Jake now had a spare chair from the garage sale, along with a coffee table. He made a playful flourishing gesture like a headwaiter as he seated Sam. He wheeled the desk chair back to the coffee table for himself and took a big bite out of one of the sandwiches. A small shower of the crispy outer crust fell as he bit into it.

"This is good!" he said.

She offered him the plastic container of carrot sticks and celery. "Eat some vitamins," she said gruffly.

"Yes, Mom," he said, laughing. "It's nice to have someone taking care of me again."

"I'm not your mother."

His eyes lifted to hers and held. "I noticed," he said, in a husky voice. Then he took a carrot stick and ate it.

Sam took a stick of celery and bit into it with a snap. What was going on here? After looking at her like that, he calmly ate a carrot! Why was she letting herself be ying-yanged around by this impossible man?

"What happened to the picnic?" he asked. "You mentioned something about a picnic when I phoned you. It didn't rain, did it?" He peered out the window at a bright, sunny day.

"Nope, that big bright ball up there is the sun, Jake. What happened is that the guy I meant to go on the picnic with was busy."

"Guy?" he asked, staring at her in alarm. Sam didn't say anything. She just stared him down. As her meaning dawned on him, a slow smile of satisfaction stretched his lips. It echoed in his eyes, which danced with pleasure.

"You mean me!" He shook his head ruefully. "I'm really sorry, Sam. I hope you didn't go to a lot of bother. You should have told me."

"I did tell you—sort of."

"You only said you were making sandwiches for a picnic. You didn't invite me to go along. I was happy you had found something to do. I thought you and your girlfriends must have set up a picnic last night."

"No, Jake, we didn't. You said you'd call."

"I did call! I put a note on the fridge to remind me." He pointed to the fridge. There was no note appended to the door. "I took it down after I called you," he explained.

He needed a note to remind him of her! This was rapidly going from bad to worse. Sam took a deep breath and said in a reasonable voice, "Since it was Sunday, I thought maybe we'd go for a drive in the country and eat by a lake or something, since—"

She stopped, wishing she hadn't added that last bit. "Since you're broke," she was going to say. And Jake's quick frown told her he was quick enough to realize it. His jaws worked silently. Since he wasn't eating at the time, she figured he was chewing on frustration.

"Since I'm too poor to buy a girl a sandwich," he said grimly.

"Woman." There was no point denying what he'd said. She could only try to distract him.

"Woman," he repeated. He set down his plate and reached across the space to take her hands. "I'll make it up to you, Sam," he said gently. "I'm just sorry we had to meet at this particular time, when I'm between jobs. I'm not really a workaholic or a cheapskate, you know. I would have enjoyed that picnic. Some place in the country, near a babbling brook." He wore a sad look as he echoed her own plans.

"Nobody called you a cheapskate! I understand, Jake. It's not a free meal or your money I'm after. I just thought you could take an afternoon off so we could spend some time together, since it's the weekend."

"I wish I could, but—" He looked with a guilty frown at his computer.

"You're busy. I'll let you get back to work."

Jake didn't say a word to stop her. He rose and gave her his hand to help her up. When they were standing, he drew her into his arms. "Thanks for coming, Sam. I really do appreciate it."

He studied her a moment, with a smile lighting his eyes, then he lowered his head and kissed her. The prickle of whiskers felt strange against her face—rough but exciting. When he pulled her closely against him, the intimacy of his body heat penetrated through his shirt. As his lips firmed for a deeper kiss, she forgot the whiskers and just reveled in the rapture of that kiss. It felt strong and real, not some romantic fantasy conjured up by moonlight or an idyllic setting. It felt like the sort of love that might come only once in a lifetime. It felt as if he meant it, and every throbbing beat of her pulse responded.

When he released her, they were both smiling in a dazed way. "I'd better go now," she said. Her voice was breathless.

Jake just nodded reluctantly. On her way out, she happened to glance at the computer terminal where he had been working. Two little stick men were on the screen.

"What's that?" she asked.

"That's the game I told you about, the Money Game."

"You were playing a computer game?" she asked.

"Well, working on it," he said. "I'd hardly call it play. There are still a few kinks to iron out." He glanced impatiently at the terminal, as if he could hardly wait to get back to it.

"Oh, I see. Well, enjoy."

Jake didn't seem to notice the sharp edge to her voice. He'd been playing a computer game! That was what was so important he couldn't take a couple of hours off to see her on a Sunday afternoon. And she, like a darned fool, had gone running after him. Never again. This was the last time she'd call on Jake Foster without an invitation.

As she reviewed their relationship, it occurred to her that she was usually the one who called on him. When had he ever actually phoned her and asked to see her? Never, except the first time, when he'd hired her to buy him a desk. Then he had the nerve to come storming in on her date with Rob, insinuating she was a wanton woman or something. As if it was any of his business!

She'd been making a fool of herself, chasing after a man who merely tolerated her. If he liked computers better than people—better than her—then let him make himself a robot girlfriend. *Woman* friend! She got into her van and ground the gears as she left.

Of course Jake didn't call that evening. She should have put a note on his fridge. He probably thought it was still the middle of the afternoon. He probably hadn't eaten any dinner either. Let him starve, the darned nerd. She had better things to do. As soon as dinner was over, she called Ginnie and Nancy and they went down to the tennis club. It was salt in the wound that her friends raved about Jake all evening, telling her how wonderful he was and how lucky she was.

"Oh, yes, he's one in a million," she said ironically.

Monday brought another disappointment. Jake called before she left for work.

"I wonder if you could do me a favor, Sam," he said. He sounded excited.

Her first instinct was to say, "Sure." As her instincts had been unreliable where Jake was concerned, she asked, "What favor?" before committing herself. She noticed that he sure remembered who to call when he wanted a favor.

"It's Beckie."

"What's wrong with her?" she asked in alarm.

"Nothing. She's fine. It's just that I have to go out of town tomorrow. I wondered if you'd come by and feed her and maybe take her for a walk."

"When will you be back?" she asked.

"Day after tomorrow, in the evening."

"You were going to leave her alone overnight?"

"I phoned Rue. She suggested maybe you wouldn't mind taking Beckie to her apartment and staying there overnight. She mentioned you'd done it once before when she was away for a weekend."

"That was the weekend, when I could afford to be away from home. I run my business out of my apartment. I have to be here during the week to take calls."

"That's why I suggested you might drop in here and feed Beckie during the day. You won't be taking calls at night, will you?"

"I also get an occasional personal call," she said. "Some of my friends do call me occasionally."

There was a long silence on the other end of the phone. Sam knew she was manufacturing difficulties. The most likely personal callers were Ginnie and Nancy. She had an answering machine, so she could leave a message to tell them where she was. It wouldn't be much trouble to drop in and feed Beckie, and she'd always enjoyed her overnight visits to Rue's sumptuous apartment, with the monster TV and great stereo. Sam just didn't want to rush in again, helping Jake, since it was possible he was taking advantage of her.

"Yes, of course," Jake said. "I didn't mean to impose. I'm sorry. It's just that something important has come up in Chicago."

Sam soon interpreted this to mean Angela had called again, probably with a more tempting offer. An offer Jake couldn't refuse or couldn't resist examining further at least.

"Chicago, huh?" Jake didn't offer any details. "I guess it'll be all right," she said coolly.

"Are you sure? I could ask the guy next door, but since Beckie and you are old friends and Rue was pretty worried, I thought maybe you wouldn't mind. Listen, just forget I asked. I'll speak to Hank. No problem."

"No, it's okay, Jake. I'll do it."

"Are you sure?"

"I'm sure."

When he spoke again, his voice sounded more natural. "Thanks a million, Sam. I'll leave the key on the ledge over the kitchen door. The dog food's in the kitchen cupboard, the leash is hanging on the doorknob. If I leave any dirty dishes in the sink, just ignore them."

"I didn't plan to wash your dishes while I was there," she said angrily.

There was another pause, then Jake asked, "Are you *sure* you don't mind doing this? You sound kind of snarky."

"I couldn't let Rue down," she said, to let him know the favor was for Rue, not him.

"Well, thanks. Can I bring you anything from Chicago? A Cubs cap, a bottle of wind from the windy city?"

Sam didn't laugh. "I do my own shopping, thanks. Bon voyage, Jake."

"See you."

It wasn't until Sam had hung up the phone that she remembered Jake had an appointment that morning with Felix Ungar, the man who ran the apartment buildings. Jake had been pretty excited about it; he thought it might lead to a few contracts. Wasn't he interested in local contracts any longer? It was beginning to look very much as if Jake had given up on Findley Falls. He was going to Chicago for a job interview. He wouldn't go to all that bother unless he was pretty serious about accepting the job.

So he planned to leave town, in other words, and hadn't even bothered to tell her. Well, why should he? They were only friends. He'd tell her in his own good time—when he had the job, when it was too late to talk him out of it. *Talk him out of it?* Where had that sneaky, selfish idea come from?

That's what was really bothering her. She wanted Jake to stay in town for *her* convenience. Never mind if he didn't have a job or any money or a decent place to stay. Of course he had to go to the interview in Chicago—but he didn't have to sound so darned excited about it. He might at least have had the decency to pretend he was sorry.

When had Jake Foster ever pretended anything? That wasn't his way. He was always upfront about things, right from the first time she'd met him, when he'd let her know he couldn't ask her out because he didn't have any money. He admitted that a woman in New York had dumped him. Most men would have kept that to themselves, out of pride.

Sam went to tend Beckie the next morning. Tuesday wasn't as busy as usual. She was glad to have something to occupy her thoughts, which had a tendency to harp on the complications, the faults and virtues of Jake Foster. A service club asked her to buy them three dozen folding chairs plus six padded chairs and a large table suitable for board meetings. As their club expanded, they were moving to permanent headquarters, with a whole house for their use. They'd be needing other items, as well. They didn't want the expense of hiring a decorator. It could be a profitable account for her if she handled the initial job well.

Sam toured every furniture outlet in the city to get the best bargain she could. During the afternoon she found time to take Beckie for a walk. She spotted Beckie through the kitchen window when she went to Jake's house to get the key. The little dog lay on the floor with her head resting on her paws, looking lonesome and dejected. Sam knew just how she felt, because she felt the same way. Beckie was so eager to get out that she brought her leash to the door in her mouth.

After their walk, Sam took Beckie back to the kitchen. She noticed Jake hadn't left any mess, after all. A few dishes had been washed and left to try on a tea towel on the counter. A note on the fridge said, "Call Felix Ungar." Sam wondered if he had remembered to do it.

Beckie went barreling toward the computer room, probably hoping that Jake was there. When Sam went after her, she saw that Jake had taken the precaution of closing the living room door to keep the dog out. Beckie whined and scratched to be let in.

"Do you miss Jake?" Sam asked, rubbing the dog behind the ears the way Beckie liked. Beckie made a low whining noise in her throat. "So do I," Sam said. "Never mind. I'll take you home tonight. You can sleep in Rue's bedroom with me. We might as well face it, old girl. We're losing him."

Beckie just barked and ran back to the kitchen. Sam filled a bowl of water for her, looked around to see that all the electricity was turned off and left.

That evening she packed an overnight bag and drove back to Alberry Drive to get Beckie before going to Rue's apartment. She took in the mail and checked the answering machine. There was nothing important enough to warrant a call to Paris. Rue phoned around eight to check that Beckie was being taken care of. Sam let Beckie bark into the phone, to satisfy Rue that all was well. Rue raved for five minutes about a boat ride she'd taken down the Seine. She had met a French movie actor, and had bought a new designer gown in hopes of getting a date with him.

Poor Rue. Poor rich Rue, out trying to buy happiness. Her apartment held every luxury money could buy. In a few years the expensive sofas and rugs would be rooted out and replaced with whatever new items the interior decorators came up with. Her clothes closets, all three of them, were bulging. Sam waded through the thick pile carpet to the window, where she looked over the lights of Findley Falls. What Rue really wanted couldn't be bought with money. She wanted someone to love, and to love her. Who didn't?

Money wasn't everything, yet people did need a certain minimal amount of it. If only Jake could have made some money in Findley Falls, he wouldn't be leaving. And she wouldn't be standing alone at this window, missing him. She felt warm tears sting her eyes and brushed them away.

The buzz of the phone interrupted her repinings. Sam's heart went into overdrive. Jake! He knew she was here. He was calling to tell her about his interview.

"Hello," she said breathlessly.

"Miss Sherman?" It was an older man's voice. It sounded vaguely familiar, but Sam couldn't place it immediately. Who knew she was here?

"Yes, this is Sam Sherman."

"Colonel Walker here. Rue Sanderson's friend. I know Rue is in Paris. I called in the hope that you were minding Beckie."

"Yes, I am. What can I do for you, Colonel?" Sam figured he'd left something in Rue's apartment and wanted to recover it.

"I'm trying to reach that young gentleman who was with you at Rue's place last week. Name of Foster, as I recall."

"Jake Foster?" Sam said. Her curious tone invited an explanation.

"Yes. I was mighty impressed with that young fellow. He had a good head on his shoulders. He's some sort of computer expert, isn't he?"

"Yes, he is. Jake's out of town at the moment."

"Pity. When will he be back?"

"I expect him tomorrow evening. Shall I tell him you called?"

"If you would be so kind. It's rather important and to his advantage." He left his number and rang off.

Sam wondered what Colonel Walker could want with Jake. His mentioning Jake's interest in computers sounded as if he was thinking of buying himself a personal computer and wanted some advice. She couldn't think what else it could be. The old colonel had a pompous way of talking. "To his advantage" probably meant he planned to pay Jake a little something for his help. It'd take more than that to keep Jake in town.

She thought Jake might phone, since he knew she was alone at the apartment. Really it seemed the least he could do. She tried to watch some TV to pass the time, but the monster screen only annoyed her. She didn't even phone any of her friends, because she wanted the line to be open in case Jake called. She flipped through a few decorating magazines while the clock on the VCR ticked away the minutes from nine to nine-thirty to ten.

At ten she gave up, had a shower, made some tea and went to bed in the guest room, which was done up in a lavish French country style. Neither the down pillow nor the silky window drapery helped her sleep. Funny how miserable you could be, surrounded by luxury. Tomorrow evening Jake would be home, and he would almost certainly tell her he had accepted a job in Chicago. She would never see him again. Maybe he would drop a postcard, but their relationship had never ripened to a point where either of them had made a commitment.

He had never said he loved her.

Chapter Ten

Since Beckie was so comfortable back in Rue's apartment, Sam left her there the next day while she went about her business. She took the dog for a short walk in the morning and came home at noon to visit her. In the afternoon, she went to the house the service club had rented to oversee the delivery of the chairs and table. The club secretary was there as agreed to pay the check.

He examined the furniture approvingly. "It looks like you've got us a good bargain, Sam," he said.

"Thanks, I'm glad you're a satisfied customer. The merchant gave me a special price when I told him it was for a service club. I expect you'll be needing other things once you move in. Desks, filing cabinets, maybe a sofa and some odd tables. You could even put a bed in one of the bedrooms upstairs—a sort of guest room for visitors," she suggested.

"We plan to do that."

"I'd be happy to undertake the shopping for you," she said.

He looked at her van and smiled. "We plan to Let Sam Do It. You can begin looking around for a fridge and stove for starters. Since we have a kitchen, we might as well use it. We can make our own coffee and keep drinks in the fridge. Cheaper than having them sent in, and more convenient."

"Is that a firm offer?"

"We're having our first meeting in our new headquarters tonight. I plan to raise the matter. I'll be in touch with you very soon. It's just a formality. You can consider it semifirm. And about the desk and filing cabinets, we'll be needing those right away, as well."

"Fine, I'll get something lined up."

It was a busy afternoon. Two of the women at the seniors' home asked Sam to buy them a new summer dress. She always gave them a very special price since they were on a limited income. She would gladly have done it free, but she knew they liked to pay their way, like everyone else. She threw in a free video this time. The video store had just gotten in a bunch of golden oldies. Ronald Coleman. Mrs. Munster loved anything with Ronald Coleman in it.

Since Jake would be home that evening to pick up Beckie, Sam decided to go back to Rue's apartment to wait for him. Dogs weren't even allowed to visit in her building. She did go home first to change, however. If this was going to be the last time she saw Jake, she didn't want him to remember her as he usually saw her, in jeans and sneakers.

She couldn't get dressed up too fancy, or he'd think she was planning to go out. She'd just wear something simple but feminine. After careful consideration, she chose a sky blue cotton dress with eyelet trim and a full skirt. Earrings and sandals lent it a touch of fashion.

Rue had invited her to feel free with whatever she could find to eat in the fridge or cupboards, which wasn't much. Neither a frozen leg of lamb in the freezer section nor a tin of crabmeat appealed to her. Neither did the bottle of maraschino cherries or capers or the tin of clams. Rue had cleaned her fridge of perishables before leaving.

Sam's suffering spirit required a heavy dose of junk food to assuage the pain. She bought two hamburgers, fries and a frozen ice-cream bar for her dinner.

"There, now I'll be fat as well as rejected," she said, and ate the two hamburgers and fries with mingled disgust and enjoyment. She left the ice-cream bar in the freezer for a bedtime snack.

Jake still didn't call. She hadn't thought to ask him exactly what time he'd be back. Maybe it wouldn't be until late. She might as well get comfortable. She propped herself up on pillows to watch the big-screen TV. It was a mystery drama, involving a woman alone in a house, being stalked by a crazed killer. Just the thing to watch when you were alone. She was glad for Beckie's canine company. The dog was something warm and living to snuggle up with, even if she wasn't much of a conversationalist.

The phone rang at ten to eleven, just as the climax of the drama approached. The psycho killer was peeking in his victim's window, drawing his knife from its sheath. Sam jumped a foot and stared at the phone, scared half to death. She lifted the receiver and said in a croak, "Hello?"

"Hi, Sam. It's me. Jake. I'm at home—finally. Sorry I'm so late. I expected to be back two hours ago.

My flight ran into a bit of trouble. I wasn't sure you'd be in, so I decided to call first. Is it all right if I pick Beckie up now?"

"Yes, that's fine, Jake."

"I'll be there in two shakes."

Since he was coming in person, Sam didn't bother to ask any of the questions that occurred to her. Questions like, "Did you accept the job?" Really that was all she wanted to know. Because if he had, that pretty well answered the other questions that plagued her.

While waiting for him to come, Sam shimmied back into her sandals, which she had kicked off to watch TV. She ran to the bathroom mirror to brush out her short hair and put on some fresh lipstick. She would offer Jake a drink. Rue kept all the fixings and had told her to help herself. She was just fighting with the ice cube tray when the buzzer sounded. Before Jake reached the door, she had got the ice cubes out and refilled the tray with water.

She ran to open the door at the first knock. She would know by the expression on Jake's face how he really felt about her. If he had taken the job and was smiling, then obvioulsy his work and money meant more to him than she did. If he'd taken the job but was glum, then maybe there was a chance they could work something out. If he hadn't taken it and was happy— that would be best of all. All these thoughts flitted through her mind in the seconds it took her to open the door.

Her eyes flew to Jake's face. He wasn't wearing any of the expressions she'd been anticipating. He didn't look particularly happy or glum. Mostly he just looked tired. He was still wearing his business suit. He had pulled his tie loose from the limp collar. The suit was slightly rumpled from the trip.

"Well, what's the news?" she demanded, even before saying hello.

"They'll let me know," he said, and walked in slowly.

"You mean they didn't make an offer after having you go all the way to Chicago? Or you didn't accept?" she added hopefully.

"The matter is under negotiation," he said.

Beckie, who had been snoozing at the foot of the sofa, roused herself to welcome Jake. While Jake played with the dog, Sam had a moment to study him. That was when she detected the air of suppressed excitement in her caller. It was there, lurking at the back of his eyes and tensing his shoulders. He wasn't moving quite naturally. When he put Beckie down and looked at Sam again, she noticed he was trying hard not to smile.

He was just breaking it to her gently. He had taken the job and was thrilled to death with it, but he didn't want to gloat.

"Can I get you a drink?" she asked coolly.

"Something tall and cold would hit the spot."

She knew Jake didn't like sweet drinks. "Scotch?" she asked.

"Do you have any beer?"

She brought two beers. "It's under negotiation, you said. You mean negotiating for more money?" she asked.

"What else? They like my work."

Sam schooled her face to indifference. "Then it's just a matter of time."

They sat on the sofa with Beckie curled lovingly at Jake's feet, looking at him with adoring eyes. Darned dog! Sam had known her forever. She had taken her to the vet and for endless walks, she had fed her bits of hamburger and taken her to be groomed, but she acted as if Jake were her only friend in the world.

"Nothing's definite," Jake said. "I've learned that lesson the hard way. Never count your chickens until they've hatched." He sipped the beer and sighed in pleasure.

Sam considered this a moment. It was good advice. She only wished she'd remembered it sooner. She'd been counting on Jake being around for a long time. Maybe as long as they both should live.

Jake said, "What's new here? Other than your dress. It looks smashing, if I forgot to mention it." His wandering look included more than her dress. It lingered contentedly on her hair and eyes, lastly on her lips. He gazed at them as if lost in reverie.

Sam found it hard to concentrate on their conversation when Jake looked at her like that. She mentioned the service club she had gotten as a customer. "Oh, and Colonel Walker wants to talk to you. He said it would be to your advantage. He thinks very highly of you. I wouldn't go buying back your watch on the strength of that, however. I think he wants you to help him buy a computer." She went and got the colonel's number from the phone pad.

Jake thanked her and put it in his pocket. "I'll give him a call tomorrow. It's a little late to do it tonight. I look forward to knowing him better. He's an interesting man."

When Sam sat down again, Jake reached his arm across the sofa and put it around her shoulders. His fingers gently massaged her nape, sending little quivers of anticipation down her spine. The excitement was glowing in his eyes more brightly than before. He asked softly, "Did you miss me?"

Sam felt like weeping. She had hardly thought of anything else but losing Jake since the moment he had phoned her last night. How could he treat it in such a cavalier manner?

She braced herself to make light of it with a joke. "I thought the day would never end. Twenty-four hours on the rack. Did he get the job, or didn't he? Will the mysterious Jacob Foster drop out of sight, leaving an irreparable hole in the fabric of life in Findley Falls?"

He grinned. "I don't think Findley Falls would miss me much if I left. Dare I hope Samantha Sherman would?"

She put on a mock noble face and said, "Life would never be the same. No more driving to 13 Alberry Drive to visit the resident genius."

"No more coffee, served in paper cups, while sitting on a door that we call a table. It was kind of fun, though, wasn't it, Sam?"

His very words told her it was all over. "Yeah, it was kind of fun." Sam didn't sniffle, but she couldn't entirely control her face. She had to pinch her lower lip between her teeth to stop it from trembling.

Jake's fingers moved to cup her shoulder in a close grip. "From now on, it'll be champagne and caviar all the way, Sam, like you're used to."

"I hate caviar. It tastes fishy."

"Fish eggs would, wouldn't they?" he said reasonably.

It seemed ridiculous to Sam that they were talking about fish eggs at a time like this. Jake could at least say he was sorry to be leaving her.

"So, when will you know for sure about the job?" she asked.

"Angela will call me tomorrow. Around three, she said. I'll call you and let you know right away. We'll go out and paint the town red if my eggs hatch as expected. I owe you. There are just a few wrinkles to be ironed out. About a hundred thousand of them," he added with a secret smile.

"You're trying for a hundred thousand dollars a year!"

"No, a hundred thousand more than they're offering. But it wouldn't be every year. I wouldn't be on salary, Sam. It's not that kind of deal."

Sam didn't know how the computer world operated. Maybe they paid their employees per job, but whatever they called their remuneration, the hundred thousand more was obviously dollars. She really couldn't blame him for accepting such a good job as that. He'd never make anything like it in Findley Falls. She couldn't even blame him for being exhilarated, after his bout of unemployment.

"I could work pretty well at my own time," Jake continued. "Fit it in with your free time, I mean, so we'd have more than an occasional walk or coffee together."

"Weekends," she said vaguely. Her weekend was really only Sunday. She worked Saturday.

Even as the crow flies, Chicago was six hundred miles away. She couldn't afford to make the flight very often, and she knew that Jake would soon tire of it if he had to do all the commuting. Since their romance hadn't reached the stage of a firm commitment, it was bound to peter out with time and separation. He'd make new friends. Why drag out the agony? It would be less painful in the long run to make a clean break and let the healing begin.

"But as I said," Jake continued, "I'm not counting my chickens yet." When he smiled down at Sam, he suddenly realized she looked exhausted. There were gray smudges beneath her eyes. A glance at Mickey Mouse's arms told him it was nearly midnight. "It's late. I'd better be going. Will you sleep here or back at your own apartment?"

"I still have my night things here. I guess I'll stay here tonight. It'll be easier."

As Jake rose, Beckie leapt to attention, tale wagging. Sam went for her leash and attached it, then accompanied Jake and Beckie to the door. Before he left, Jake's hand went to his pocket. He drew out a smaller modern version of his Mickey Mouse watch.

"Chicago was all out of wind," he said. "I bought you this instead, to remind you of me and the hard times."

He took Sam's right wrist and attached the watch. She already wore a better watch on her left wrist. "Thanks, Jake. You didn't have to buy me anything." She didn't especially want any reminders of this painful episode in her life. That's all it was going to be, just an episode.

"I wish it were studded with diamonds," he said, gazing at her. "Or at least had a chain linking it to mine."

"That doesn't sound very convenient," she said, smiling dutifully.

"Love isn't always convenient. It comes and hits you in the face at the damnedest time."

The word *'love'* was like a red alert signal to Sam. Her eyes flew to Jake's. He was looking at her watch. When he looked up, he wasn't smiling. He looked sober, almost grave. The moment stretched for what seemed a long time, while Sam waited for him to say something more.

"I'll call you tomorrow, Sam. Thanks for taking Beckie." The grave look softened to longing as he stood in the darkened doorway.

"That's all right. I enjoyed it."

"Why don't you drop in tomorrow whenever you're free? I'll be home all day."

Sam felt she had done more than enough dropping in on Jake. If he wanted to see her, he knew her phone number. He knew where she lived. She might get there only to find him with his head buried in the computer terminal, wondering what day it was.

"You said you'd call me after three, after Angela notified you about the job," she reminded him.

"But three o'clock seems so long to wait. I'll need something to sustain me."

He pulled her into his arms for a long, passionate kiss. Sam never wanted it to end. How could he kiss her like that and not love her? "Love isn't always convenient", he had said. And this time it was just too inconvenient to last. He still hadn't said, "I love you." He hadn't even said "We'll overcome the inconveniences." He just kissed her until her insides were awash in warm syrup, then left.

The next morning Sam dressed and went back to her apartment to wait for the phone to ring. Just when she badly needed a diversion to help her forget Jake, her phone was deathly silent. Maybe Jake was right, and she was wasting her talents trying to make a living by doing people's shopping for them in a small city like Findley Falls. Surely Chicago needed professional shoppers, too. No reason she couldn't move there if Jake... He hadn't even suggested she do that. It had never occurred to him. He obviously wasn't as keen on their being together as she was.

By ten o'clock she still hadn't had a single call. She decided to begin some tentative looking around for the service club. That took her through the rest of the morning. At noon she didn't feel like going back to her empty apartment, so she had a sandwich at a corner drugstore.

Sam often had lunch there. The waitress with the name Rosie embroidered on her pocket knew Sam well, and Sam knew Rosie Tucker had a husband who drove a truck, two children, and she was saving for a house.

"The usual?" Rosie asked.

It was kind of nice to be known around the city. Sam was beginning to feel she had found a home. Why should she leave it to go to a huge city where she didn't know anyone? Of course she would have gone in a flash if Jake had suggested it, but since he hadn't... She'd built up a good customer list. She had good friends here. She liked Findley Falls.

Sam nodded. "Yes, please."

A toasted Western and a glass of milk were soon placed on the counter before her. The waitress leaned over the counter and said, "Me and my husband just bought a new house, Sam, out at the west end of town."

"Oh that's great, Rosie. I'm glad to hear it."

"We decided to strike while the mortgage rates were down. If you happen to come across a deal on carpet, let me know. I'd like to do the whole downstairs in pale beige and the upstairs in a dusty blue. We'll need a few other things, as well. Mind you, we're a bit tight for money now. I thought maybe the secondhand stores—but I don't have much time to look around."

For Sam, the words *a new house* were like the starting bell for a race horse. Before she left the drugstore, she had a list of ten items and a ballpark figure of what she could spend. Looking for the items took her through the afternoon until three o'clock.

Sam didn't want to hear the news that Jake was leaving town on her car phone. That could be hazardous to her driving, so she drove back to her apartment. The red light on her answering machine told her she had had a call. She pressed the button and heard Jake's voice.

"Sam, it's Jake. Call me as soon as you get in. Good news!"

Her heart sank. He sounded so happy he could hardly control himself. So he had gotten the outrageous price he demanded. He must be good! She should be happy for him, but love was selfish as well as inconvenient. After a click, Jake's voice spoke again. "It's noon. Why aren't you home having lunch? *Call* me." Another click, and Jake spoke a third time. "Where are you when I need you, woman? You're not in your van. You're not at home. This is an urgent APB on Sam Sherman. Be on the lookout for a white minivan, side panel bearing the words Let Sam Do It."

She could hear the rising impatience in Jake's voice. He'd been phoning her all day. Angela must have phoned earlier than she'd said she would. Sam went to pick up the phone, then hesitated, trying to compose herself to let on she was happy for Jake.

While she sat looking at the phone, it rang, startling her. She lifted the receiver. "Hi. Sam here."

"Sam, about time!" It was Jake, again.

"I just got home. I got your messages on my machine. I was about to call you."

"A good thing. I was about to call out the state police. You'll never guess what!"

"Tell me."

"I called Colonel Walker. He wanted a meeting right away. The son-of-a-gun is on the board of directors of that corporation that owns all the apartment buildings in Findley Falls. I guess I made a good impression. I got the contract! Six apartment buildings! With six satisfied customers—and you can be sure I'll see that they're satisfied—I can sell that program to a computer software company."

"That's great, Jake. Did you hear from Angela yet?"

"Not yet. She said she'd call soon after three. I'd better hang up. Don't want to miss the call. I knew you'd want to hear."

"Thanks for calling. I'll let you go now."

Sam wasn't sure what the logistics would be for selling the condo program. Presumably Jake would have to be available for consultation, since he was so determined to see his customers were satisfied. Her heart lifted a little. He had said the job for Angela's firm wasn't a strictly salaried job. Maybe he meant to spend some time in each city.

The phone rang again before Sam had left the phone table. It was a young working mother, a doctor, who wanted a fancy imported Aprica English baby carriage for the baby she was expecting in a month. She also wanted a lot of other expensive items—crib, dresser, layette. Money didn't appear to be any object. The woman also told her three of her friends were expecting, all of them much too busy to do their own shopping. "It's the biological clock thing," the doctor explained. "We decided it was time to factor in a child."

Sam's head was spinning. This was the kind of customer who made so much money she hardly had time to blow her own nose. This was a vast, untapped market, just waiting to be developed. In the old days they were called Yuppies. Those of them who still enjoyed that life-style were willing and able to pay for it.

Yes! She was going to do all right in Findley Falls. She went searching for the latest newspaper to check for sales at the baby stores. If she could firm up those other three mothers-to-be, she could swing a very special price on four Aprica baby carriages. If she hadn't been so anxious to receive Jake's call, she would have dashed downtown immediately.

Since Jake had mentioned going out to paint the town red, Sam went to her closet instead and began to look over her dresses. She was holding a rose-colored dress up to her in front of the mirror, trying to decide whether it clashed with her red hair, when the phone rang. She threw the dress on the bed and flew to answer it.

"Congratulate me," Jake exclaimed. "I did it! I'm solvent. Yippee!" His euphoria lent him an unaccustomed air of playfulness. She wondered if Jake was like that when he wasn't so troubled as he'd been recently. She had never seen him in all his moods.

Sam felt far from euphoric. The blow was cushioned by knowing Jake was also committed to the condo program. She forced herself to say "Congratulations!" with some semblance of enthusiasm.

"I'll be right over."

"But it's only three-thirty. You said something about dinner—"

"I can't wait. I have to kiss somebody. Beckie doesn't quite fit the bill."

"All right, come on over," Sam said, smiling in spite of herself.

"I just left."

Sam figured it'd take Jake fifteen minutes to arrive. She freshened up, but didn't bother to change. Presumably they'd both change before going out for dinner. Fifteen minutes passed, twenty, thirty, and still no Jake. Sam called him, but there was no answer. Now what could have happened? He had been so excited he might have had an accident. Visions of Jake, crippled for life, with his nice car wrapped around a telephone pole, came to frighten her. When he finally arrived forty-five minutes after calling her, her fear found an outlet in anger.

"What happened to you? What took you so long? I was afraid you'd had an accident."

"Sorry I'm late. I had to arrange a few things," he said, placing an apologetic kiss on the corner of her lips.

She could see it wasn't himself he had arranged. Jake was wearing his usual shirt and jeans. The peck on the lips softened her anger. "You said something about wanting to kiss someone," she reminded him. She took his hand and led him into the apartment.

"Control yourself, woman," he said with mock sternness. "There's a time and place for things. I've chosen the place. Just grab that suitcase you call a purse and let's go to it."

Sam assumed he had set something up at his house. Maybe champagne. She didn't want him to know she had guessed the surprise, so she just got her purse. When they were in the car, Jake didn't head for Alberry Drive, but for the country.

"Your house is that-a-way, Jake," she said, pointing back over her shoulder.

"I know. You don't think I'm taking you to that dump, now that we're rich?"

We're rich. She especially liked that *we,* that instinctively included her in his life. "So, what dump are you taking me to?"

Jake's head turned. Oh, lord, I've offended him again, she thought. She was just about to apologize when she saw that he was grinning. "You'll see," he replied. "But remember, curiosity killed the cat." He waited a moment, then said, "You're supposed to say 'Curiosity brought it back'. I see you need some lessons in the art of cliché."

"And you're just the guy who can give them."

"If you've got it, flaunt it."

The car sped out of town, headed roughly south west. The only place Sam could think of was Syracuse. Maybe Jake wanted to celebrate in some bigger city.

"We should have changed if we're going to Syracuse," she said.

"We're not going to Syracuse. Why would we go to Syracuse?"

"Well, where are we going?"

"Think of the past, Sam. Think of my selfish—er, make that self-absorption— No, delete that whole bit. I don't want you concentrating on my many faults at this point. Just think of what I owe you. That should keep you busy for a couple of hours." His chuckle was infectious. She had never seen Jake so effervescent.

"You owe me dinner and a can of red paint to paint the town," she said.

"I knew you were a literalist. Think green, not red." He turned to her again. His grin had turned to a soft, contented smile she hadn't seen before. "Green for trees and grass," he said.

Since Jake was being mysterious, she decided to relax and let him enjoy it. She'd find out where they were going in good time. He kept looking out the window as the car sped along. "Where was it you planned to go for that picnic on Sunday?" he asked.

"There's a kind of miniforest a couple of miles farther on, with a brook. It's a government nature park. You can walk in it without annoying any farmers or without danger of being shot by hunters." So that's where they were going. A funny place to go to celebrate.

Jake kept looking out the window. When he saw the rough-hewn sign, he drove into the parking lot and got out. He helped Sam out of the car, then went to the trunk and took out a big wicker basket.

"We're going to have that picnic," he explained.

"That's nice, Jake." That was very nice. Much nicer than a public restaurant, with people watching.

Jake carried the basket as they walked hand in hand along the path. Around them, soaring pines seemed to touch the azure sky, where a few puffs of white cloud hung suspended, like a picture on a postcard. The path was slippery with fallen needles. A scent of pine and resin and moist earth rose as they disturbed the fallen needles. Scuttling, furtive noises of wild creatures in the underbrush sounded loud in the vast, hovering silence. An occasional bird song warbled in the treetops high above.

Jake stopped once and gazed up at the treetops, etched against the sky, their tips furred with golden sunlight. "It's beautiful, isn't it?" he said softly. "I'm glad we have it to ourselves today, but why aren't people here, enjoying it?"

"Because they're still at work. There are plenty of people here on the weekends and in the summer, when they're on holidays."

"Poor, unfortunate souls, working on a day like this. Nine-to-five grind. Maybe you were wise to have avoided it, Sam. It must be kind of fun, doing all sorts of different things as you do."

"Like I said, it suits me. I'm glad you've finally realized I'm not an underachiever."

"That wasn't what I thought. After I got over feeling sorry for you for being exploited, I thought you were just doing it for kicks. A rich girl's hobby, if you like. Poor little rich girl, so lacking in imagination she couldn't do anything but shop."

"I'm not a rich girl. I'm just a fairly well-off man's poor daughter."

"You're rich in the things that count," he said. "In friends, generosity. A rich little poor girl, maybe."

"Woman," she said.

"No, no. I'm the authority on clichés. It's poor little rich girl, not poor little rich woman."

"The stream is this way," she said, turning to the right.

They heard its gurgling ripple before it came into view. It was concealed behind a stand of cedars. Crystal-clear water flowed over a bed of pebbles worn smooth by time. There were no benches or tables. Those were located closer to nearby Lake Oneida. Other than not having a blanket, the picnic promised to be much as Sam had planned for last Sunday.

The warm sun shone on them, removing the nip from the fresh June air. The soft grass, spangled with wildflowers, was their blanket. Jake opened the basket and arranged a white tablecloth on the ground. He took out various plastic containers holding cold chicken, salads, fruit, cheese and lastly, a small cake. It was choclate, ornately decorated with chocolate flakes and cream and cherries.

"A veritable feast!" Sam laughed. "You went to a lot of bother, Jake."

"I confess, I didn't make it myself."

"Do tell. And here I thought you had roasted up a chicken and baked a cake in half an hour. So this is what kept you late." She got out dishes and cutlery. "Shall I carve the chicken, or do you want to?"

"You carve. You can just cut off a leg for me. Meanwhile, I'll do battle with this cork." He took a bottle of champagne from the basket.

It had been several hours since her sandwich lunch, and although it was a few hours before her usual dinnertime, Sam discovered the fresh air and the walk had sharpened her appetite. The delicious lunch was made more enjoyable by Jake's high spirits. He poured champagne in tulip glasses and proposed a toast.

"To us," he said simply, touching the lip of his glass to hers with a gentle clink. His eyes, meeting hers over the glasses, gave meaning to the simple toast. They seemed to say that she and Jake were a team, that neither a job nor time nor distance nor money, nor the lack of it, would ever change that most important fact.

"I'll drink to that," Sam said.

She passed him a plate and they both helped themselves to the feast Jake had brought. The picnic in the open air was more enjoyable than the gourmet food at the Napoli Garden. They began exchanging stories from their childhood. Jake's had been more difficult than hers, of course. He had taken a paper route to save money to buy a bicycle. His eyes still shone when he spoke of it. He had worked in a supermarket on Saturdays during high school to make spending money and to save for college. He wasn't complaining; he was just telling Sam about himself.

She told him about her early days, too. She noticed that while his childhood memories involved people, hers involved things: the toys her parents had given her to take their place. Her dad her given her her first bicycle when she was six. It hadn't meant anything, except that her parents were going to Europe that summer. Maybe that was why she liked her job so much. She was with people all day long.

When they were finished with the chicken and salad, Jake took a knife to serve the cake.

"I never met a woman who doesn't like chocolate torte," he said. "Or are you an exception?"

"I'm a chocoholic," she said, passing her plate. "Give me a big piece."

While they ate their cake, Sam said, "You haven't given me the details about your job in Chicago, Jake." Strangely she had forgotten all about it while they had been exchanging childhood reminiscenses.

She sensed that he had been holding it off as a surprise. That air of suppressed excitement she had first noticed the night before still hung about him. Since she already knew he had got the job, the surprise must be the salary.

"Oh, I didn't take the job," he said offhandedly. "I turned that down before I went to Chicago."

"You didn't accept the job! Then why—"

"No, I didn't want to leave Findley Falls. I went to Chicago to sell them our Money Game—for quite a lot of money. If it does well, we'll get more royalties. This way, I'll have plenty of free time to work on other games as a hobby. Well, a working hobby. With luck I'll come up with other games I can sell. I'll have to spend some time with the condo software people, too, of course. That's the route I've decided to take—work free-lance. What do you think?"

"Is that what you meant when you said we'd work it out? I thought you meant you'd visit on weekends or something."

"I sort of misled you, accidentally on purpose," he admitted. "It was nasty of me, but I wanted to get confirmation from Angela first. Give you the whole enchilada for a surprise. So, what's your opinion?"

Her radiant smile told him her answer. "Just leave a couple of minutes of your time for me, huh?"

"You're top priority, Sam. I decided that while I was gone, too. Whether they took the game or not, I didn't plan to leave Findley Falls—and you. It's taken me too long to find you."

"Shucks, I never even knew I was lost," she said, but she said it with tears of joy in her eyes.

"Isn't it lucky I came along to let you know these things?" he asked, folding her in his arms. She felt his lips nibbling at her ear. When he spoke, his voice was husky with longing. "I love you so much, Sam."

"Oh, I love you, too, Jake. I thought I'd never hear you say it. Why didn't you tell me sooner?"

He gazed down at her happy face. The love reflected there made him feel humble, unworthy. "How could I ask you to marry me when I didn't have a job or any immediate prospects? I wanted to have something to offer you. That's why I've been working so hard."

"I wouldn't have minded living on Alberry Drive."

"I would have minded asking you to. Here I've been cursing fate for the gift of love, just because it didn't come at exactly the right moment. I should have been on my knees giving thanks. It isn't the timing that's so important after all, is it?"

"No, and it isn't the money, either, although that's convenient, of course."

"I've been happier struggling along in that dingy house, going for walks with you and having coffee, than I ever was when I had money to burn. It was your rich dad that gave me the idea you were probably a material girl."

"Until I realized how much money I'd wasted, I guess I was kind of a material girl. *Woman!*"

"Woman," he agreed. "*My* woman," he added softly. He gazed at her for a long moment, as if to memorize her face for all eternity. Then he lowered his lips to seal the commitment.

The silent forest seemed to echo with celestial bells. The old familiar excitement curled, ready to spring. But beneath the tension Sam felt a sensation of deep, abiding peace. He loved her. That's all she ever really wanted. In the depths of the silent forest, the wind moved the tall treetops. It caressed the embracing couple benignly as it blew across the meadow, carrying the first warmth of summer.

* * * * *

**HE'S MORE THAN
A MAN, HE'S
ONE OF OUR**

DADDY'S ANGEL
Annette Broadrick

With a ranch and a houseful of kids to care for, single father Bret Bishop had enough on his mind. He didn't have time to ponder the miracle that brought lovely Noelle St. Nichols into his family's life. And Noelle certainly didn't have time to fall in love with Brett. She'd been granted two weeks on earth to help Brett remember the magic of the season. It should have been easy for an angel like Noelle. But the handsome rancher made Noelle feel all too much like a woman....

Share the holidays with Bret and his family in Annette Broadrick's *Daddy's Angel*, available in December.

Fall in love with our **Fabulous Fathers!**

FF1293

Take 4 bestselling love stories FREE

Plus get a FREE surprise gift!

Special Limited-time Offer

Mail to Silhouette Reader Service™

3010 Walden Avenue
P.O. Box 1867
Buffalo, N.Y. 14269-1867

YES! Please send me 4 free Silhouette Romance™ novels and my free surprise gift. Then send me 6 brand-new novels every month, which I will receive months before they appear in bookstores. Bill me at the low price of $1.99* each plus 25¢ delivery and applicable sales tax, if any.* That's the complete price and—compared to the cover prices of $2.75 each—quite a bargain! I understand that accepting the books and gift places me under no obligation ever to buy any books. I can always return a shipment and cancel at any time. Even if I never buy another book from Silhouette, the 4 free books and the surprise gift are mine to keep forever.

215 BPA AJH5

Name	(PLEASE PRINT)	
Address	Apt. No.	
City	State	Zip

This offer is limited to one order per household and not valid to present Silhouette Romance™ subscribers.
*Terms and prices are subject to change without notice. Sales tax applicable in N.Y.

USROM-93R ©1990 Harlequin Enterprises Limited

UNDER THE MISTLETOE

Where's the best place to find love this holiday season? UNDER THE MISTLETOE, *of course! In this special collection, some of your favorite authors celebrate the joy of the season and the thrill of romance.*

#976 DADDY'S ANGEL by Annette Broadrick
#977 ANNIE AND THE WISE MEN by Lindsay Longford
#978 THE LITTLEST MATCHMAKER by Carla Cassidy
#979 CHRISTMAS WISHES by Moyra Tarling
#980 A PRECIOUS GIFT by Jayne Addison
#981 ROMANTICS ANONYMOUS by Lauryn Chandler

Available in December from

Silhouette
ROMANCE™

SRXMAS

The miracle of love is waiting to be discovered in Duncan, Oklahoma! Arlene James takes you there in her trilogy, THIS SIDE OF HEAVEN. Look for Book Three in November:

A WIFE WORTH WAITING FOR

Bolton Charles was too close for comfort. Clarice Revere was certainly grateful for the friendship he shared with her son. And she couldn't deny the man was attractive. But Clarice wasn't ready to trade her newfound freedom for love. Not yet. Maybe never. Bolton's patience was as limitless as his love— but could any man wait forever?

Available in November,
only from

SRAJ3

Share in the joy of a holiday romance with

1993 SILHOUETTE Christmas STORIES

Silhouette's eighth annual Christmas collection matches the joy of the holiday season with the magic of romance in four short stories by popular Silhouette authors:

LISA JACKSON
EMILIE RICHARDS
JOAN HOHL
LUCY GORDON

This November, come home for the holidays with

where passion lives.

SX93

When the only time you have for yourself is...

Christmas is such a busy time—with shopping, decorating, writing cards, trimming trees, wrapping gifts....

When you do have a few *stolen moments* to call your own, treat yourself to a brand-new *short* novel. Relax with one of our Stocking Stuffers— or with all six!

Each STOLEN MOMENTS title is a complete and original contemporary romance that's the perfect length for the busy woman of the nineties! Especially at Christmas...

And they make perfect **stocking stuffers**, too! (For your mother, grandmother, daughters, friends, co-workers, neighbors, aunts, cousins—all the other women in your life!)

Look for the STOLEN MOMENTS display in December

STOCKING STUFFERS:

**HIS MISTRESS Carrie Alexander
DANIEL'S DECEPTION Marie DeWitt
SNOW ANGEL Isolde Evans
THE FAMILY MAN Danielle Kelly
THE LONE WOLF Ellen Rogers
MONTANA CHRISTMAS Lynn Russell**

HSM2

SILHOUETTE.... Where Passion Lives

Don't miss these Silhouette favorites by some of our most popular authors!
And now, you can receive a discount by ordering two or more titles!

Silhouette Desire®

#05751	THE MAN WITH THE MIDNIGHT EYES BJ James	$2.89	☐
#05763	THE COWBOY Cait London	$2.89	☐
#05774	TENNESSEE WALTZ Jackie Merritt	$2.89	☐
#05779	THE RANCHER AND THE RUNAWAY BRIDE Joan Johnston	$2.89	☐

Silhouette Intimate Moments®

#07417	WOLF AND THE ANGEL Kathleen Creighton	$3.29	☐
#07480	DIAMOND WILLOW Kathleen Eagle	$3.39	☐
#07486	MEMORIES OF LAURA Marilyn Pappano	$3.39	☐
#07493	QUINN EISLEY'S WAR Patricia Gardner Evans	$3.39	☐

Silhouette Shadows®

#27003	STRANGER IN THE MIST Lee Karr	$3.50	☐
#27007	FLASHBACK Terri Herrington	$3.50	☐
#27009	BREAK THE NIGHT Anne Stuart	$3.50	☐
#27012	DARK ENCHANTMENT Jane Toombs	$3.50	☐

Silhouette Special Edition®

#09754	THERE AND NOW Linda Lael Miller	$3.39	☐
#09770	FATHER: UNKNOWN Andrea Edwards	$3.39	☐
#09791	THE CAT THAT LIVED ON PARK AVENUE Tracy Sinclair	$3.39	☐
#09811	HE'S THE RICH BOY Lisa Jackson	$3.39	☐

Silhouette Romance®

#08893	LETTERS FROM HOME Toni Collins	$2.69	☐
#08915	NEW YEAR'S BABY Stella Bagwell	$2.69	☐
#08927	THE PURSUIT OF HAPPINESS Anne Peters	$2.69	☐
#08952	INSTANT FATHER Lucy Gordon	$2.75	☐

```
            AMOUNT                                    $ _____
DEDUCT:     10% DISCOUNT FOR 2+ BOOKS                 $ _____
            POSTAGE & HANDLING                        $ _____
            ($1.00 for one book, 50¢ for each additional)
            APPLICABLE TAXES*                         $ _____
            TOTAL PAYABLE                             $ _____
            (check or money order—please do not send cash)
```

To order, complete this form and send it, along with a check or money order for the total above, payable to Silhouette Books, to: *In the U.S.*: 3010 Walden Avenue, P.O. Box 9077, Buffalo, NY 14269-9077; *In Canada*: P.O. Box 636, Fort Erie, Ontario, L2A 5X3.

Name: _____

Address: _____ City: _____

State/Prov.: _____ Zip/Postal Code: _____

*New York residents remit applicable sales taxes.
Canadian residents remit applicable GST and provincial taxes.

SBACK-OD

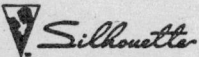